I0546569

WHERE THERE'S FAITH

Fairfield Corners

Book 3

L.A. REMENICKY

Lavish Publishing LLC

Contents

First Edition

Fairfield Corners Series Book 3

All Rights Reserved

Published in the United States by Lavish Publishing, LLC, Midland, Texas

Paperback Edition

ISBN: 9781944985288

Cover Design by: Wycked Ink

Cover Images: Adobe Stock

www.LavishPublishing.com

Acknowledgments

I'll try to keep this short—bear with me!

Finally! For a while, I didn't think this book would ever get finished. Approximately eighteen months after I started the first line, it's finally done. I went through a serious writing slump for a year and then released three books within four months.

Now that this one is complete, it's on to the next...

Thanks to Karen Loomis, bestie extraordinaire, for being there and listening to me rattle on about my characters and for being my Alpha Reader. You will always get to read everything first! And thanks to my Beta Reader, Diane Martin—your suggestions were spot on!

Special shout-out to MJ Symmonds for winning my title the book contest! I love this title!

And, thanks to Lavish Publishing, LLC, for believing in me and my books—we are going to do big things together!

L.A.

Chapter One

Unfazed by the pounding on the door, Robbie rubbed the sandpaper over the wood, enjoying the rhythm of the song and the satiny smoothness of the wood under his hands. Creating handmade memory boxes out of blocks of wood soothed his soul better than the oblivion he had tried to find at the bottom of a whiskey bottle.

Music blasted through his workshop and its open windows, his way of shutting out the world that no longer had *her* in it. His attention was focused on this special container for his soon-to-be niece or nephew; he still needed to find the right design for the lid. Ragan had cried when he gave her the one for Skylar with the guitar and music notes carved into it.

The rumble of his stomach convinced him it was time to stop for lunch. He grabbed his shirt off the hook by the door, marveling at the seventy-degree day in October in northeast Indiana. According to the forecast on the news earlier that day, the weather would turn more seasonable later that afternoon, bringing in the cold and rain.

The change in temperatures brought thoughts of Thanksgiving. He grimaced at the idea of the holiday in a few short weeks; it would be his first big family holiday since that day back in May when he had hit rock bottom and almost died.

Pulling the door open, he stepped back just as a woman fell towards him. He frowned while grabbing her arms to keep her from collapsing inward, the contact with her skin stirring something he wanted to keep buried. His hands dropped to his sides when he was sure she was steady. "What do you want?" he said with a scowl as he crossed his arms. "Well? I'm waiting."

"Hi," she said as she stuck out her hand. "I'm Faith McMillan. I'll be staying next door for the next few months."

"I've got things to do. Did you come here for a reason?"

She frowned at his brusqueness. "I just wanted to ask you to turn down the music a couple of notches. I'm trying to work, and it's distracting me."

"No." He crowded her out the door and closed it behind him. Striding toward his house, he turned and saw her standing there with her mouth hanging open. "This is private property; I suggest you leave."

He watched as she stomped back to the Romero's. Just what he didn't need, a beautiful distraction. At least, when the weather turned, he wouldn't be subjected to the sight of her in those shorts with her long, tanned legs that seemed to go on forever. Maybe she would stay indoors where she wouldn't disturb him.

After a quick lunch of a sandwich and chips washed down with a bottle of water, he swept up the wood shavings, lost in thought about the intrusion into his life. Why would someone want to be on the lake this time of year? She must be friends with the Romeros because they never rented out their lake house. And what was with the sunglasses? He hated when he couldn't see someone's eyes; it felt like they were hiding something.

He shook his head, vowing to forget about the feel of her skin under his hands. Fate had taken away his chance at happiness in a fiery explosion on a California freeway. Even her name felt like a kick in the stomach—that was the moniker they had picked out for a girl. The chestnut color of her hair was similar to Madison's, making him want to grab fistfuls of it and bring it to his nose to see if it smelled the same.

After straightening up his workshop, he headed back to the house. The memories followed him as he turned on lights and prepared a chicken to roast in the oven. The recollections wouldn't stay away, taking with them his appetite and tempting him to down a bottle of whiskey to drown them out. The news playing on the television couldn't keep his attention as he ate, allowing the images a chance to invade his thoughts, bringing an overwhelming sense of loss and grief.

With the chicken feeling like a lead ball in his stomach, he walked out onto the deck, reveling in the feel of the wind biting into his skin. His hands gripped the railing as if to anchor him in the present as the memories took him back. He watched the scene play out on the back of his eyelids as he lifted his face to the moon, trying to change the outcome as he sank to his knees and sobbed for the life that was ripped from him.

Robbie looked on as he kissed Madison goodbye, screaming at himself to stop her. He had been so worried about that deal with the east coast branch that he let her walk out the door and drive to the airport by herself, telling her he would catch a later flight and meet her that night in Indianapolis before heading for Fairfield Corners the next day to introduce her to his family. Eloping to Las Vegas the weekend before had been a spur of the moment decision made after they discovered she was pregnant. They kissed and he handed her the keys, not knowing he would never see her again.

Two hours later, he had just finished up his conference call and was dialing his cell phone to call a cab when he heard a knock on the door. One of the two LAPD officers at the door asked him if he owned a 2012 Mustang, and he knew his life was over. A gasoline tanker truck had blown a tire and lost control on the highway right in front of his car, causing a massive pileup as it exploded, engulfing his car in flames.

He had to find a way to live without her. She was gone. Forever.

Turning to whiskey, it had dulled the pain…temporarily. At first, he only drank on the weekends to fill the emptiness in his soul. When that wasn't enough, he started drinking during the week after work, but it eventually turned into sneaking alcohol during business hours.

Anything to dull the ache. Going home to Indiana had never even crossed his mind as he continued to plod through his life, usually inebriated, always hopeless.

After three years of trying to get through to him, his boss couldn't ignore the situation any longer. He gave Robbie an ultimatum: get help or he was fired. By this time, Robbie no longer cared about his job, so he left. He gave away his furniture and packed up what was left of his life. Putting on a happy face, he called his twin sister in England because he didn't want to show up at his parents' alone. He suggested they both go home for their anniversary, vowing to start fresh once he was with them all. That didn't work out quite like he thought it would. His sister was reunited with her true love; and he was happy for Ragan but despaired, wondering if he would ever be truly happy again. His drinking continued, and three months later he almost died.

Despite a night of tossing and turning, he was awake before dawn the next morning. The wind rattled the storm windows and whistled through the trees, almost convincing him to skip his morning run. Reclaiming his life had included getting back into shape. This aerobic exercise and his afternoon workouts helped keep his ghosts at bay, so he rolled out of bed and pulled his sweats out of the closet.

Twenty minutes later, his breath plumed a white vapor in front of him as he set out on his customary five-mile run. His first attempt after being released from the hospital had been a walk of about one mile and made him almost puke as his body adapted to this new life without alcohol. With shoes slapping against the pavement, he let his mind wander back to the enigma that was his new neighbor.

Remembering how she blushed after almost being plastered against his naked chest made him smile. His conscience prickled at how he had treated her. His mother would lay into him if she ever found out about it. His only excuse was his bad mood, brought on by a phone call from a friend in Los Angeles.

He cleared his mind as he ran down the country road that wound around the lake—a five-mile loop that was perfect for his run.

Chapter Two

Faith trudged up the front steps of the Romero's cottage wondering about the man next door. "I hope I don't need his help with anything. What a grouch," she mumbled to herself as she closed the window, hoping to muffle the music coming from next door, but it was still too loud for her to concentrate. She pondered about the jagged scar that started at his eyebrow and traveled down to his cheekbone, highlighting the pain in his gray orbs. As she attempted to clear her mind, the apparition she had come to think of as her muse appeared. "He will be important, keep trying," she said.

Knowing she was always right, Faith resigned herself to getting past his gruff manners. "Just what I need," she mumbled as she squinted at the laptop open on the desk. The pain in her head thumped to the beat of the bass blasting from next door. "Great, now I won't get anything written today." She closed the computer's cover and tiptoed downstairs, wobbling slightly as the pain made her nauseous and threw off her equilibrium. The headaches were the last of the physical reminders of the night three years ago when her life had changed.

She found her prescription bottle and took a painkiller before stumbling her way to the bedroom. Rubbing the pendant of her necklace between her fingers, she closed her eyes and concentrated on the neck-

5

lace and what it signified. The piece of jewelry, the only clue to her identity, swayed as she held it in front of her face. As always, she pondered the significance of the moon and star design and of the numbers five and thirteen engraved on the back. The pounding in her head intensified as she set the necklace on the dresser before stumbling to the bed and the welcome oblivion of sleep.

Faith woke to her cell phone buzzing across the nightstand with an incoming call. She hated the way the pills made her groggy, but they were better than the alternative: blinding migraines that lasted for days. The headaches were coming less frequently. She hadn't had one for almost a month before today.

She pulled on her sunglasses before opening the blinds. Phone in hand, she walked into the kitchen to make some coffee. As the beverage brewed, she checked her phone and smiled when she saw the missed call was from her friend Nikki. With her phone in one hand and the other wrapped around a steaming coffee mug, she walked out onto the deck to watch the sun set over the lake.

"Hey, Nik," Faith chirped up after hitting redial.

"You were supposed to call me when you got to the cottage. I've been worried."

"Sorry, it was so beautiful and peaceful I was itching to get some writing done. For some reason, it felt like I was home. Unfortunately, things didn't work out that way."

"What happened, sweetie?"

She toyed with her hair, not wanting to admit how much the encounter with the neighbor had affected her. "The guy next door has been blaring rock music loud enough to wake the dead. He was a real grump about it when I asked him to lower the volume, too."

"Hmmm...the Newlins must have rented out their cottage. Doesn't sound like Robbie."

Faith laughed. "Whoever he is he's gorgeous, but his personality could use some help." The breeze blew some leaves around the deck, bringing a chilliness that wasn't there earlier. "It's starting to cool off. I need to go in and see if I can get anything written now. I'll call you in a couple of days." As always, she wondered if she should tell Nikki

6

about her muse. Perhaps it was a manifestation caused by her brain injury. Too late this call, maybe next time.

Talking to Nikki had brought the mystery man back into her thoughts. She wondered what his story was as she imagined running her fingers through his hair, the blond streaks mixed in with the brown indicating he spent a lot of time out in the sun. Maybe he would end up in one of her books someday with some tragic backstory of heartache and loss.

She shivered, the cool breeze blew harder and smelled of rain, heralding more seasonal weather was on the way. Closing the window, she heard when he finally turned off the music. His choice of entertainment wasn't what bothered her, it was the volume. She loved a good rock song, especially one by Adam Bricklin, but she couldn't tolerate the booming bass when she was trying to work. Blocking out the music made it harder to concentrate and seemed to set off a headache.

The black clouds rolling through brought in the night early, creating shadows within the room. As the brightness of the sun was dimmed by the clouds, she could remove her sunglasses, revealing the faint tracing of scars from the surgeries to recreate her face. In her current mood, she knew she wouldn't be adding much to her most recent work in progress. It would have to be the story of her rebirth and rescue that day three years ago.

She opened the file and started to type, transported back to that day she woke up with no memory of who she was and worse, no recognizable features. She was found beneath an underpass, beaten and bloody with no identification and no recollection of her life. A broken necklace in her pocket was the only connection she had.

Brushing away a tear, she wrote about the feelings of helplessness and despair. As the days turned into weeks and no one came forward looking for her, she'd sunk into depression and self-loathing, wondering what was so bad about her that no one cared. Whoever attacked her had broken all the bones in her face, destroying any hope of recreating it back to the way it had been. The itch to write was the only thing that kept her going through those dark days of pain and therapy, both physical and mental. Well, that and the voice of her muse.

The doctors patched her up, but they could not restore her memory. She searched the face of everyone she met, searched for something that would spark a memory. She built a life, managing to write a best-selling novel while she healed. The money was enough to pay some of her hospital bill and support her frugally while she worked on another book.

The doctors and nurses had become her friends during the long days spent in the hospital as her injuries healed. Nikki, the Intensive Care nurse who spent so many hours with her while she was helpless and depressed, became her best friend. She lent her the laptop computer that was her gateway to coming back to life through her writing and opened her heart and her home. When she offered Faith the use of her family's lake cottage for the winter, Faith jumped at the chance to be off on her own. Nikki said the small fishing lake was peaceful in the fall and winter, and the few homes on the shore closed up for the season. It was just what she had wanted, private and secluded.

The man next door was the only thing spoiling this perfect place. She remembered the feel of his hands on her arms, the warmth that seemed to reach into her soul, igniting a fire that she wasn't ready to deal with. Her new face made it feel like she was a teenager, unsure of herself and her sexuality. She had obviously been in some type of relationship; she had miscarried as she lay in that alley being beaten with a baseball bat. *Why did no one come looking for her? Had she been running from a bad relationship?*

The chiming of the clock brought her back from the past, reminding her that it was time to think about dinner. She threw a frozen dinner in the microwave, wondering why she didn't know how to cook. That would go to the top of her list for tomorrow when she went to town: buy a cookbook.

Chapter Three

Faith looked up from her laptop at the sound of a car pulling up the driveway next door. She had planned to drive to Fairfield Corners that morning, but a plot element had popped into her head, so the story took precedence. If she didn't get it out "on paper", it would disappear forever. The black Escalade parked and beeped the horn. "Great, they're just as noisy as that guy living in the house," she grumbled, her focus totally gone.

As her computer shut down, she watched a pretty blonde ease out of the vehicle, her pregnancy apparent. Grumpy guy walked out of the house and smiled before hurrying over and pulling the woman into his arms for a hug and a kiss. He opened the back door, and after a couple of moments straightened up with a young boy in his arms and a radiant smile on his face.

"No wonder he was a grump, he was waiting for his wife to return." Faith sighed and closed her laptop. She wondered if she would ever find someone to share her life with. Shaking her head, she told herself to get over herself. No one would want a woman without a past.

The slam of a car door brought her back to the present, gazing out the window at the neighbor carrying a box towards his house. He looked up and stared in her direction as if he could see into her thoughts.

She stepped back and grabbed her coat and purse on her way out the door, forcing the memory of his tortured gray eyes out of her mind.

~

Robbie watched out the front window at her car driving away as he picked a card and moved his piece to the next yellow space on the board. Skylar clapped his hands. "My turn now, Unca Robbie?"

"Yes, Sky. Pick a card, bubba." He helped his nephew figure out where to move his piece, his thoughts turning to "what if". What if Madison hadn't died that day? Would he have a child with Skylar's blond hair playing the game with them?

"Hey, you okay, Robbie?" Ragan asked, concern showing on her face. "How are you doing living out here by yourself?"

"I'm good. It just hit me that our child would be about the same age as Skylar. I was just wondering what if."

"You will be a great dad someday. You don't get just one chance. Look at me, I've been lucky enough to love and be loved by two wonderful men. I did love Liam, and I was heartbroken when he died, and then there's Adam." She stared off into space with a smile on her face.

"I don't know. It just feels like Madison was "the one" and that I missed my chance for happiness." He ran his hand through his hair, pushed the "what if" thoughts away, and tried to concentrate on the game with his niece and nephew. "Your turn, Jenna."

Ragan lowered herself onto the couch, sighing. "I know it's hard, but you can move on. Just remember what your therapist said. You need to get back out into the world."

"I know. Can we talk about something else?" He looked up at his sister, frowning at the tiredness he could see in her eyes. "Hey, you feeling okay? You seem tired. Why don't you lie down? The kids and I can find something to do while you take a nap."

"I am tired. It's exhausting growing a human being," she smiled as she rubbed her belly. "I quit taking new photography jobs last week. There's only two left for me to finish up and then I'm done until after this one is born."

Robbie pulled the blanket off the back of the couch and covered her, kissing the top of her head. "Just rest, sis, I've got this covered." He helped Skylar put the game pieces back in the box and put it away in the closet. "Hey guys, want to help me with the memory box I'm making for your new brother or sister?"

Skylar bounced up and down in excitement. "I'll take that as a yes from you, bubba. Jenna? You want to help, too?"

"I'd rather stay in here and read my book, if that's okay."

"Sure, sweetheart. What are you reading?"

Her eyes lit up at his interest in her book. "It's *Muse* by Erin McFadden, and Aunt Cassie said the author lives over in Huntington and that she'd try and get her to come do a signing at the bookstore. Isn't that awesome?"

He pulled her in for a hug. "Go read your book. Let me know if you or your mom need anything. Sky and I will be out in the workshop."

Faith walked into The Book Ends Here and stopped to take it all in. A short counter to the right of the door held a cash register, shelves of books stood straight ahead with chairs and couches scattered throughout the store, inviting her to grab one of the copies and start reading.

The scent of coffee tickled her nose, bringing her attention to the refreshment bar at the left side of the store. She looked over the menu and ordered her favorite Chai Tea Latte, hoping it would be as good as the coffee place near Nikki's out in Los Angeles. The first sip confirmed it—it was even better.

Remembering her promise to herself, she found the cookbook section and frowned at all the choices. How in the world would she be able to pick one?

"Hi, I'm Cassie. You look like you could use some help."

Faith looked up from the cookbook in her hand and smiled. "Yes, how could you tell? I'm Faith McMillan."

"You look familiar. Have we met before?"

"No, not that I remember."

"Well then, it's nice to meet you, Faith. You look just a bit overwhelmed. What kind of recipes are you interested in?"

"I want a good basic cookbook so I can teach myself how to cook. The thought of making something more complicated than a grilled cheese sandwich terrifies me."

Cassie plucked a book from the shelf. "This one has some simple recipes with clear directions."

Faith flipped through the book. "Looks good, I'll take it. Can you tell me how to get to the closest grocery store?"

Cassie gestured with her left hand as she rang up the cookbook. "Head east on Main and turn left on Maple. It's one block down on the left." She handed Faith the receipt and a pen along with her debit card for her signature. "Where are you staying? Karen didn't tell me about any new renters."

"I'm staying at a friend's house out on Little Beaver Lake."

"You must be staying at the Romero's. Robbie mentioned something about it. Wait a minute. Are you the Faith McMillan who wrote *The Highlander's Lass*?"

"Yes, that's me," Faith replied with a blush. Someone recognizing her name from her book didn't happen often, so it was still a shock.

"We'll have to schedule a book signing while you're here."

"So, is Robbie the guy in the blue two-story? I introduced myself yesterday, he wasn't very nice. Maybe he'll be in a better mood now that his wife's back." She hurried towards the door, her anxiety ramping up. "I'll call you next week to set up a signing." Faith walked out the door, not seeing the look of confusion on Cassie's face.

Settling her sunglasses on her face she breathed in the crisp winter air as she strolled to her car. The snow was beautiful but she was not a fan of the cold temperatures. Sliding into the driver's seat, she was surprised to find that the car was still relatively warm. After turning the heat on full blast, she motored out of her parking space and onto the road.

If she hadn't had a death grip on the steering wheel, the car would have shot across the road into the other lane. She had just turned up the volume on the radio when her favorite Adam Bricklin song started playing. "Dreaming of you," she sang, her eyes riveted on the snow-covered road in front of her. Driving in snow was new to Faith, and she drove cautiously. The thump of the flat tire jogged something in her memory, and she was transported to another time and place. Staring out the windshield, she saw a different landscape than the deserted road she was on.

"Dreaming of you," Faith sang as she drove along the highway. The thump of a flat tire made her think how lucky it was that she was at an exit. She pulled off the freeway…"

Her mind cleared, and she was stopped on the side of the road, the car tilted slightly to the right. The memory was just a flash of a moment in time, but it was something. Maybe after three years, she was finally beginning to remember. Uncurling her fingers from around the steering wheel, she got out of the car to change the flat.

Faith stared at the reason for her unexpected stop as pain hit behind her left eye, piercing and sharp. "Great," she muttered as she pulled the keys out of the ignition. *I'm on the lake road, maybe I can get this tire changed and make it home before it gets too bad. Usually, I have time to take my meds and block most of the pain.* The stabbing feeling increased as she walked towards the back of the car and the nausea hit as she tried to unlock the trunk. *Wow, the pain is getting bad quickly this time. Could it be because of the memory?*

The sun glinted off the chrome of the bumper into her eyes, blinding her. She felt her way to the side of the car and dropped to her knees, everything she had eaten that day coming up. Crawling around the steaming mess, she found the shade from the car and collapsed onto the gravel, her head resting on her knees. The cold seeped through her jeans as the agony she was experiencing blocked out everything else.

The sun glaring off the rear window caught his attention long before he could make out the car. He jogged closer, wondering who was out on the lake road this time of year. He crossed the street and noticed the car was tilted toward to the right, wondering whose car it was and where they were—it was highly unlikely that anyone had stopped and picked them up.

The pile of vomit turned his stomach, reminding him of his destructive days when he would drink until he was sick and then drink some more. He turned the key in the lock on the trunk, opening the lid to see if the spare was gone. It was still tucked into its spot, ratcheting up his anxiety. *Who would leave their car out here in the middle of nowhere with the door open and the keys hanging off the trunk?*

Gravel shifted, and he then heard the sound of retching.

"Hey, you okay?" Robbie asked as he walked around the back of the car avoiding the discarded stomach contents.

Faith looked up, her hand shakily wiping at her mouth. "Yeah, leave me alone. I'm fine."

"You don't look fine." Robbie took her hand and pulled her up, frowning when she swayed drunkenly. He wondered why she thought she needed to drink at two in the afternoon. "Go lay down in the back seat. I'll get the tire changed and drive you home."

He opened the door and waited for her to crawl in, the pallor of her skin making him wonder how much she had ingested. A trip to the emergency room may be the next order of business.

After stowing the flat and the jack in the trunk, he drove her home. He handed her the keys, noticing that her color was slightly better.

"Thank you. I'm sorry you had to go to so much trouble," she said as she turned toward the house, the quick movement throwing her off balance.

Robbie caught her as she swayed. Bending at the waist, his arm went behind her knees, and he lifted her into his arms.

"Put me down. I can make it into my house on my own," she mumbled, her words slurred. "Why did it have to be the grumpy guy from next door?"

Ignoring her protests, he took the keys from her hand and let them into the house, striding across the living room to the bedrooms. "Which room are you using? The master?"

At her mumble, he turned into the master bedroom and set her down on the bed. "Do you have a nightgown or something? I'm sure you don't want to sleep in your smelly clothes."

She fell back onto the pillow, her breathing even and steady. "Thanks," she whispered as sleep took over.

"Dammit, I can't leave her like this." He rummaged in the dresser drawers until he found a pair of flannel pajama pants and a long-sleeved t-shirt. Shaking her shoulder, he tried to wake her enough to help him get her changed. No luck. She was completely out, and it looked like nothing short of a nuclear blast was going to wake her. Starting with her shoes, he undressed her and poured her into the pajamas.

Knowing from experience how she would feel when she woke up, he set a glass of water and a bottle of aspirin on the nightstand and a plastic wastebasket next to the bed just in case. Feeling like a creeper, he dug her phone out of her purse and sent himself a text so he would have her number. Brushing her bangs off her face, he hoped that she would find the strength to admit she had a problem and get some help.

Going a step further, he took her dirty clothes down to the washer and started a load of laundry. Satisfied that there was nothing else he could do, he walked back to his house, locking the door behind him. As he strode across the driveway, he wondered what had driven her to drink.

Faith rolled over and opened one eye just enough to look at the clock. The pain spiked briefly at the slight movement, settling back to a constant dull ache when she lowered her head back onto the pillow. *How did I get here?* The last thing she remembered was crawling into the shade of the car after the pain had made her sick. The faint smell of vomit wafted to her nose from her hair. *Gross.*

How did I get into my pajamas? Reaching toward the nightstand,

15

she felt around and grabbed her phone, frowning when she couldn't find her sunglasses. Squinting, she turned on the power, hissing when the light hit her eyes. The text message icon glowed, letting her know that she'd missed a message.

Got u home and into bed. Clothes in washer. When you're ready there are AA meetings. Robbie aka Grumpy Guy From Next Door.

AA meetings? Oh God, he thinks I was drunk. Still squinting, she sent a text back.

Thanks. Faith.

The light from the phone's screen felt like it was searing her retinas. She turned it off and dropped it on the nightstand before closing her eyes and surrendering to sleep once again.

Chapter Four

The Monday before Thanksgiving dawned cold and crisp, the sun shining brightly. By eleven, clouds had rolled in bringing the threat of freezing rain. Robbie cursed under his breath as he worked to get the lug nuts loosened on the front tires of his car. After almost running his vehicle through the front window of Cassie's bookstore the day before when the brakes slipped, he knew he needed to replace them. His favorite radio station blared out of the speakers as he pulled the calipers off the car.

Humming along with the song on the radio, he thought about Ragan and the imminent arrival of his niece or nephew. Ragan had said everything was fine when she visited on Friday, but he still worried. An odd feeling came over him as he opened the box containing the new brake pads. *Quit being a worry wart, she's fine. Ragan's the one who knows when things happen, not you.*

The first brake pad was installed, but he couldn't ignore the worry any longer. Searching the work bench for his phone, he remembered he'd left it in the house on the charger. Forgoing his coat, Robbie sprinted across the driveway to the door, shivering at the cold wind blowing in from the north.

His phone buzzed with a notification as he walked over to the counter. *Ten texts and six missed calls over two hours? Shit, this can't be good.*

Listening to the voice mails, he grinned at Adam's message: "You're going to be an uncle today. We're headed for the hospital. Meet you there!" Realizing it had been two hours since that first call, he grabbed his keys before he remembered that his car was in the garage with the brakes disassembled.

"Shit." Dialing Adam's phone, he hoped he could talk someone into coming out to get him.

Adam answered, "Where the hell are you? Ragan is freaking out that you're not here. This baby is coming fast. You better be on your way."

"I'm leaving right now. Tell Ragan I'm on my way."

Robbie grabbed the key to his motorcycle off the rack by the door. "Not ideal, but it'll have to do," Adam grumbled.

Rolling the bike out of the garage, he wished he had gotten around to installing the electric starter. He jumped on the kickstart lever with no luck. *This bike better turn over, or Ragan is going to be pissed. Hell, I'll be pissed. I couldn't be there for Sky's birth; I don't want to miss this one.*

Standing at the kitchen sink drinking her tea, Faith looked out over the lake and smiled. Peace and quiet were helping her get the story in her head out onto her laptop.

She had surpassed her word count goal for the morning, so she decided it was a great time to take a break and go check the mailbox. Nikki had told her that she should be receiving a package within the next couple of days.

Deciding to skip putting on her coat, she hurried out the door, shivering when the wind cut through her clothes. *Not stopping for my jacket wasn't such a bright idea.* Pulling the mail out of the mailbox, she was pleased to see the box from Nikki had arrived.

A string of curse words brought her attention from the mail in her hand to Robbie trying to start the bike. Not even her surly neighbor could put her in a bad mood today. She watched as he kicked his helmet, smiling at the inventiveness of his cursing.

"Hey, neighbor. Need some help?" She decided that since he had helped her get home last week, she could attempt to be friendly. She did owe him one.

Robbie looked up, a smile appearing on his face. "Actually, yes. I need to get to town like five minutes ago. Ragan's in labor, my car is torn apart, and I can't get my bike to start. Can I bother you for a ride?"

Thinking about how good-looking he was when he smiled, his mention of labor brought home the fact that he was off limits. Pushing the lustful thoughts out of her mind, she smiled. "Sure. Let me grab my keys and my coat."

Pulling her car out of the garage, she jumped at the knock on her window. "I'm really in a hurry. Do you mind if I drive?"

"That might be best. I'm not even sure how to get to the hospital." Sliding over, she looked over at Robbie as he folded himself into her car, surprised at the butterfly feelings in her stomach. *Get a grip, he's married.*

"Thanks for this. You have no idea how much I appreciate it."

"I owe you for making sure I got home safely last week and washing my clothes."

Turning his attention to the road, he stepped on the gas and turned left toward town.

Unsure of herself, Faith stared out the window and thought about the storyline of the book she was writing. As she plotted out the next chapter, she began to imagine Robbie as the main character; his looks seemed to fit. Lost in the world inside her head, she didn't notice the time flying by as they sped toward Fairfield Corners.

Careening into the hospital parking lot with a squeal of the tires, Robbie pulled into a parking place and shoved the shifter into park. Sprinting up the sidewalk, he dropped the keys in his pocket and held open the door. "You coming?"

"I thought I would just head home. I don't want to intrude, and I'm sure you can find a ride home later."

"It's starting to snow. Do you have any experience driving in this crazy mess?"

"Well, not really. I'm from California."

"That explains why you ran out to get the mail with no coat. Come on, I'll have someone drive you home later."

"Uh, okay, I guess."

Robbie motioned her inside. As she walked past him, he took her hand, lacing his fingers with hers. Pulling her behind him, he hurried up to the registration desk. "Hi, Lisa. What room?"

"Room three on the second floor. You better hurry. Adam's been down looking for you every fifteen minutes."

"Thanks."

Robbie strode down the hall, dragging Faith along behind him, not noticing how she was finding it difficult to keep up with his long strides.

The elevator doors opened as they walked up, and Adam looked relieved to see them. "Damn, Robbie, way to cut it close. I was just going to give you a call again. She's asking for you, screaming actually. She insisted she was going to wait to have this baby until you got here."

Robbie grinned at the look on Adam's face—part wonder and part terror. "Lead the way. Adam. This is Faith McMillan; she's staying in the Romero's cottage. Faith, this is Adam Bricklin."

They exited the elevator before Faith could reply. Robbie and Adam took off running. Faith stood there in the middle of the hall, unsure of where to go. She tried to wrap her head around the fact that she just met Adam Bricklin face to face in a small hospital in Fairfield Corners, Indiana.

What am I supposed to do now? Robbie has my keys. I guess I'll find the waiting room.

"Faith, hi. What are you doing here?"

Faith turned and saw Cassie from the bookstore. "I gave Robbie a ride. His car wasn't running, and he needed to get here."

"I'm glad he finally made it. Ragan was stressing herself out about him not being here. Come on, I'll introduce you to everyone."

"Oh, okay. Can I ask you something first?"

"Of course, go ahead. I'm sure we have some time before the baby makes an appearance."

"Why doesn't Robbie live with Ragan? As worried as he seems today, I would think he wouldn't want to be away from his pregnant wife."

Cassie laughed. "I think there's been a misunderstanding. Why do you think Robbie and Ragan are married?"

"I saw how he treated her when she came for a visit last week. And the boy, he looks like Robbie, except for the eyes."

"That explains the comment you made at the bookstore as you were leaving. I wondered about that. Skylar looks like Robbie because he is his uncle. Robbie and Ragan are fraternal twins, and Ragan is married to Adam Bricklin."

"Oh my God, I'm so embarrassed." Faith looked down at the floor and let her hair hang over her face to hide the blush on her cheeks.

"Don't worry, I won't tell anyone. Come on, they don't bite."

Faith's mind was whirling with all the names. It looked like half the town was in the waiting room.

"And here comes Logan, my husband." Cassie looked at him with such love on her face. "Hey, Dudley, this is Faith McMillan. Faith, this is my husband, Logan. He's one of the county deputies."

"He's related to Adam, isn't he? He's got the same eyes."

"Yes, they're cousins."

"I'm never going to remember everybody's name. Wait, why did you call him Dudley?"

"Stop by the bookstore next week and I'll tell you the whole story." Cassie stopped when Robbie stepped into the waiting room.

"It's a boy! Mother and baby are both doing great!"

The room erupted into cheers as Robbie tried to get everyone to quiet down. "Ragan and Adam thank you all for your support today. He will be out shortly to announce the name they've chosen, and he'll have some pictures."

21

Faith sat alone on the couch trying to be inconspicuous during this time of celebration. She hadn't actually met Ragan, and up until a few minutes ago, she thought Ragan was Robbie's wife.

The couch creaked as Robbie sat down next to Faith. "Hey, you okay?"

"Yes." She turned and looked at him, smiling in response to the goofy grin on his face. Staring down at her hands, she started to apologize for her assumptions. "I want to apologize for…"

"For what? You haven't done anything wrong."

"I need to apologize for what I was thinking about you."

"You were thinking about me? After the way I treated you the day you moved in?" Robbie put his finger under her chin and brought her face up, so she was looking him in the eye. "I want to explain about that. You caught me at a bad time. I have some issues that I'm working through, and it was a bad day."

"Okay, as long as you let me apologize for thinking that you and Ragan were married." Faith's cheeks turned pink as she remembered how much the idea of Robbie being married had bothered her.

"That's a first," Robbie chuckled. "I've never had anyone think my sister was my wife before. Tell you what, let's start over from this moment." He stood and pulled Faith up with him, positioning her at arms-length. "Hi, I'm Robert Newlin," he said with his hand held out for her to shake.

"This is silly."

"Just humor me, please."

"Oh, okay." She wiped her hands on her jeans before taking his hand. "Hi, Robert. Pleased to meet you. I'm Faith McMillan."

"See, now we can forget about everything that happened before." He looked down at her, wondering how two people in his world could have those same whiskey-colored eyes.

Adam walked into the room with his phone in his hand. "Hey, everyone, I've got pictures. Ragan is exhausted and says that Adam, Junior will be at the Thanksgiving feast at The Corner Pub on Thursday."

"While you have the masses entertained with the pictures, I'm going to go see AJ," Robbie said to Adam. "Come on, Faith, time for you to meet my sister."

"Oh, no, I couldn't. This should be family time, and I don't want to intrude."

"Get over here already," Robbie said with a smile. "I want to show off my new nephew. Besides, Cassie let it slip that you wrote that book that Ragan loved. She'll be excited to meet you."

Robbie smiled at Faith's blush. It still amazed her that someone wanted to meet her just because she wrote a book. "If you insist."

"Yes, I insist." He took her hand and strode down the hall.

"Slow down. My legs are a lot shorter than yours."

"Oh, sorry. I just can't wait for you to meet Ragan," he said with a chuckle. "She wants to express her appreciation for you getting her knuckleheaded brother here in time. Those are her words, not mine."

"I think I'm going to like your sister. I can't believe you were going to ride your motorcycle in this cold. You would have been a popsicle by the time you got here."

Robbie pushed the door open and stepped through, pulling Faith with him. "Hey, sis, this is Faith McMillan. She's the reason I made it today. And, she wrote that book you were nuts about last summer."

"Hi Faith," Ragan said with a grin, looking up from her hospital bed with the baby in her arms. "Thanks for making sure this brother of mine was where he was supposed to be today." She grinned at Robbie as he looked at his feet.

"Come closer and meet Adam, Jr." She gently brushed her fingers over the light hair on the baby's head. "Robbie, the nurse was supposed to bring me some more water. Can you please go find her and remind her?"

"Sure, Ragan." He smiled at Faith as he walked past her and out the door.

Ragan sat up straighter in the bed. "I want you to give my brother a chance. He told me about how he treated you when you first met, and I want you to know he normally isn't such an ass. He's been through a lot, and I just want to see him happy."

"What? How did you get the idea…?"

23

"I'm sorry, I must have misread the way you were looking at him. Please, forgive me. Ever since Adam and I got back together, I seem to have this insane idea that everyone around me needs to be part of a couple to be happy. Let's just put it down to pregnancy hormones and forget about it."

Faith stepped closer to the bed. "It's not that I'm not attracted to him, but I have my own problems I'm working through, and it wouldn't be fair to him to subject him to my issues." She looked down at the floor. "Not that I didn't enjoy being plastered up against his chest." She looked up and saw the smirk on Ragan's face. "Oh my God, did I just say that out loud?"

Ragan laughed. "I won't tell anyone. Just be his friend. I worry about him being out there at the lake by himself all the time."

Faith's cheeks were still red when the sound of the door opening brought her attention to Robbie walking into the room.

She thought she saw a look of desire in his eyes before his attention went to Ragan. "I'll just let you two have some time…" she said as she backed up towards the door, uncomfortable being the center of attention.

Another step back, and she ran into Robbie. She trembled when his hands wrapped around her upper arms. Breathing faster, she tried to quell the feelings of helplessness and fear.

"Hey, it's just me." Robbie let go and stepped around, so he was facing Faith. "I'm sorry if I startled you."

"It's okay. For some reason, if anyone grabs me from behind, I start to freak out. I wish I knew why." The concern in Robbie's eyes made her want to step into his arms and hold on tight.

Ragan looked from Robbie to Faith. "I hope you'll join the crowd on Thanksgiving at the pub. I have a copy of *The Highlander's Lass* that I would love to have you sign."

"I don't think I'll be able to make it. Nikki is flying in on Wednesday, and we are going to her grandparents down in Indianapolis. Maybe next time."

"That's too bad," Ragan said with a smile. "We'll have to make

24

plans to get together some other time." She yawned. "Robbie, go make sure Faith gets home. I'll see you tomorrow."

Robbie kissed AJ on top of his head before laying another on Ragan's cheek. "Love you, sis. I'll see you tomorrow."

Faith's heart clenched, wondering if she would ever get to have a family. The door closed softly behind her as she quietly walked out of the room. Brushing a stray tear off her cheek, she turned around at the sound of Robbie walking up behind her.

"Hey, why'd you run off so fast?"

"Just giving you some privacy. Can you take me home now? I need to work on my book today, and it's getting late."

Robbie jingled the keys in his pocket. "Okay. Just let me tell Adam we're leaving." He stepped into the waiting room, leaving Faith alone in the hall.

She pulled out her phone and checked her messages, anything to keep from thinking about a family. *How could she have a family when she didn't even know who she was?* Just a couple of texts—one from her agent and one from an unknown number. To be sure it wasn't something important, she opened the one from the unknown number. Her hand shook when she read it: **I will find you.** She deleted the message, looking around to be sure no one had seen her.

Faith spent the drive back to the lake trying to push the look of concern in Robbie's eyes out of her head. She didn't want anyone to feel sorry for her, even if they didn't know about her memory loss.

Pulling into Faith's driveway, Robbie put the car in park. He had known the exact moment she fell asleep because something about her pulled at him. She looked so peaceful that he was reluctant to wake her. He didn't like the shadows he saw in her eyes when she thought no one was looking. *What put those shadows there? And why did she freak out when I put my hands on her arms from behind her?*

He leaned back in the seat and sighed, tired from the excitement of the day and tired of being alone. What was it about her that made him want to open himself up to her? Somehow, she was able to chip away at the ice he had built around his heart without even trying.

Chapter Five

Swiping the mascara wand over her eyelashes, Faith's excitement grew as she anticipated picking Nikki up at the airport. She didn't have to hide her condition from her friend; she could be herself.

Her thoughts turned to meeting Robbie's sister Ragan the day before. The yearning for a family of her own had flared up as she had stared at AJ in the hospital. He was such a sweet baby. She knew she wanted a family. A husband and child would be enough.

Determined to stop living in a past she couldn't remember, she removed her necklace, staring at the pendant with the numbers engraved on the back. What do the five and thirteen mean? She would probably never know.

"You can do this," Faith whispered as her shaking hand placed the necklace in a heart-shaped porcelain box on the dresser. Time to look forward instead of back.

Her phoned chimed, reminding her it was time to head to the airport.

∼

27

Faith stood in the baggage area watching the monitors. When the status of Nikki's flight changed to "Arrived", her excitement grew.

Faith's phone buzzed with a text.

Just landed. Are you here?

She hastily typed her reply.

Yes, can't wait to see you. Feels like it's been three months instead of three weeks.

Time slowed to a crawl as she waited for the rapid clicking of Nikki's heels on the tile floor. Not even the chapter she had brought with her to edit could keep her attention.

Shoving the printout into her bag, she stood as Nikki came into view—her height making her hard to spot. Five feet tall without the stilettos on her feet, she was dwarfed by most of the people around her.

"Faith! You look good. Lake life must be agreeing with you." Standing on her toes, they embraced. "I've missed you. No one else I know in Los Angeles will watch old Looney Tunes cartoons with me." Nikki hugged her again. "That's from Penny. She misses her Aunt Faith."

"Has the situation with Stephen improved? Any chance you will get shared custody?"

"Unless I can get something on him to use as leverage, nothing will change. Can we talk about something else? We can't fix that situation today, and it's making me miss Penny."

"Let's grab your bag and get out of here. I've got so much to tell you."

"What, did you finish the book already? I knew the quiet would help you get some work done."

"It's quiet, that's for sure. But no, I haven't finished the book yet. I did have some excitement a couple of days ago."

Nikki was practically bouncing up and down in her seat as Faith pulled out onto the highway. "So, there was some excitement on Little Beaver Lake? You must be joking."

"Nope, I'm totally serious. I told you about the good-looking guy next door? Turns out, he is Robbie Newlin. I don't know the whole story, but he just got out of rehab six months ago, and now lives out at the lake by himself."

"Something must have happened when he was out in California. We used to meet up for dinner every couple of months. Last I talked to him, over three years ago, he had a girlfriend and was doing well at work. I wonder what happened?"

"I don't know. He told me he's working through some issues but didn't mention what they were."

"So, you said there was some excitement a couple of days ago?"

"Yesterday, I looked out the window and saw Robbie frantically trying to start his motorcycle, which was odd as it was only thirty degrees outside and it looked like snow. I could see him cussing and kicking at the bike, so I ran over to see if I could help."

"So...you forgave him for being a jerk that first day?"

"Yeah, I did. He treats me like a friend one day and then like he can't stand me the next." Faith's full attention went to the road as she merged onto the highway. As soon as she was up to speed, she set the cruise control.

Nikki checked her lipstick in the mirror as she prodded. "And...go on. You've got my attention."

"Robbie was frantic. He needed to get to town as Ragan was in labor, but he was in the middle of replacing the brakes on his car and couldn't get his motorcycle started. I felt sorry for him, so I offered to drive him to town."

"That sounds like Robbie. He was late for class a lot in high school because he got distracted working on his car or bike."

"Anyway, I got him there just in time. Cassie chatted with me while we waited, and I was so embarrassed to discover that my assumption was totally wrong." Faith was glad she had to keep her attention on the road. "I thought Robbie and Ragan were married."

"What?" Nikki yelled before laughing hysterically. "You thought Robbie was married to Ragan? Oh my God. How did you get that idea?"

"Never mind; forget I mentioned it."

"Hmmm... So, enough about Neighbor McHottie. How are you? Get any more strange texts?"

Faith stared out the windshield at the road ahead. "No. Must have been a wrong number. They seem to have stopped." She hated lying to Nikki but didn't want her to worry.

"Good. They were getting a bit creepy."

Faith was glad to pull into the drive at the cottage. It had started to snow. Not enough to cause any problems, but it put her on edge. Talking about the threatening texts she had received increased her anxiety. Who was it, and what did they want?

Nikki laughed, snorting with glee.

Faith looked over at her. "What? Those texts aren't funny."

"I was just thinking of the look on Robbie's face when I call him Neighbor McHottie." Saying it out loud made her laugh harder.

"Don't you dare," Faith cried. "I'll die of embarrassment if you do."

Chapter Six

The noise hit her first as she stepped into the pub. The murmur of voices and a song playing on the jukebox competed for her attention. She smoothed a non-existent wrinkle out of her skirt as she looked around the room. Nikki's grandmother was under the weather, so they were attending the Thanksgiving dinner at the pub instead of driving to Indianapolis as originally planned.

Spotting Robbie sitting by himself, she watched as people stopped to talk with him, a couple of the men clapping him on the back.

The smile that spread across his face when he looked up and saw her standing there made her heart beat faster as she looked down at the floor.

"Faith, you came," Robbie exclaimed as he pulled her into a hug. "I'm glad."

His arms encasing her pushed away the feelings of insecurity; they felt like home. For the first time since she woke up in that hospital bed, she wasn't worried about her past.

He pulled her along as he made his way to the other side of the room and stopped in front of a handsome man who was staring at Ragan with a wistful look on his face. "Hey, Mark. I want you to meet Faith McMillan. She's staying in the Romero's cottage for the winter.

"Nice to meet you, Faith."

She wondered about the way Mark looked at Ragan. She wished Robbie looked at her like that.

Robbie left, leaving Faith to talk to Mark alone. "So, Robbie tells me you're an author. What do you write?"

Faith smiled and mumbled, "Historical romance. Nothing you would want to read."

"You'd be surprised. I started reading romance when I was an intern—I would read any book left behind to stay awake during a slow overnight shift. To be honest, there are a few authors that I buy for my e-reader."

She giggled at the thought of this handsome guy, who was definitely book boyfriend material, reading romance novels. "I'm sure I'm not on that list. My first book was published last spring."

"Wait… Faith McMillan. I knew your name sounded familiar. You wrote *The Highlander's Lass*. I'm impressed. I really enjoyed it. After Cassie raved about it for weeks, I downloaded it. I'll have to buy a paperback copy so I can get you to sign it."

Faith blushed. "I have some promotional copies; I'll make sure you get one. No reason you should have to buy it twice. I'm just glad you enjoyed it."

Mark took his phone out of his pocket. "Do you mind?" At Faith's nod, he pulled her in close to him and snapped a picture.

Robbie stared as Mark pulled Faith into him and took a picture, unwanted feelings of jealousy flickering within him. *She's not mine. I have no reason to be jealous. She's not my girlfriend.*

Turning to get away from the sight of them laughing together, he noticed Adam clapping someone on the back. He looked familiar, and Robbie attempted to figure out why as he walked towards them. *Holy crap, that's Fletch Carmichael. I forget that Adam is Adam Bricklin. To me, he's Ragan's husband, not a rock star.*

Meandering across the room for a refill on his soda, he motioned to

Mike, who happened to be behind the bar filling a pitcher of beer. "Thanks, man. I'm sorry you have to work tonight."

"I'm not. This is a great party. I don't mind serving the drinks, and I get to have Thanksgiving dinner with my friends. A win-win in my book."

"If you need a break let me know."

"I don't think I'll be counting on you to cover me. Ragan would have my head if I let you behind the bar," Mike said with a smile.

"I just meant I would find someone to cover for you, not that I would do it myself. It's only been six months. I know I'm not ready for that kind of test yet."

The slam of the door echoed over the buzz of conversation and brought his attention to the short, buxom brunette hanging up her coat near the front entrance. From the back, he could see her rounded behind and the stiletto heels on her shoes. *I know only one person that could be.* "Hey, Romero, do you need a stepstool to reach the coatrack?"

"Funny, Newlin."

He picked her up and swung her around as he hugged her. "How are you, Nikki? And how's Penny? You didn't bring her with you?"

"I'm good. Penny is with her dad this weekend. I'll have her on Christmas Day. Can you believe she's going to be six next month?"

She whipped out her phone and started showing him the latest pictures of her daughter. "She's growing like a weed. How are you, Robbie? We haven't talked for quite a while."

The sadness he'd been trying to keep out of his mind crept into his eyes. "Sorry I quit calling. Something happened and I checked out for a while."

"A while? Three years is more than a while. What happened?"

"I guess I do owe you an explanation. You want a drink?"

"Sure. A beer would be great."

Robbie motioned to Mike for a beer. At Mike's frown, he grinned and walked up to the bar. "Not for me, for Nikki."

"Tell her I said 'hi' and to stop and talk with me if she has time."

"Sure thing."

With Nikki's beer in hand, he headed to the table. "Here you go, Nik. You told me about Penny, but how are you?"

"I'm fine. I'm getting tired of the traffic out in L.A., but I love my job at the hospital." She sipped her beer and frowned at the sadness in Robbie's eyes when she mentioned his old stomping grounds. "What happened, Robbie?"

"I met the love of my life and got married but she was taken from me."

She grabbed his hand and held on tight. "I'm so sorry, Robbie."

"When Madison discovered she was pregnant, we had a quickie wedding in Vegas over the weekend. That Monday, we were going to fly out from LAX to come here so she could meet my parents and tell them the good news."

He sipped at his soda, wishing it was whiskey to drown out the memories. "I got a call from the office that the deal I was brokering with a company on the east coast was stalled. Workaholic that I was, I sent Madison on without me, intending to catch a later flight and meet her in Indianapolis."

Without letting go of his hand, Nikki moved her chair closer to his and reached up to brush the hair out of his eyes. "You want to talk about this later?"

"No," he exclaimed, looking around to see if anyone had heard him. He swallowed hard, concentrating on keeping his breathing even. "You remember that accident on the 405 where the gas tanker truck jackknifed and caught that car on fire? That was my car, and the driver was Madison."

He took a deep breath to keep his emotions under control and let it out slowly before continuing. "For three years, I drank until I passed out to drown out the memories. That was a dark time in my life, and I'm not proud of the way I handled it. Six months ago, I cut myself up pretty badly while I was out of it and almost died. That was my wake-up call."

Nikki brushed away the one tear he let escape. "My God, Robbie, I'm so sorry."

"Enough about that. It's Thanksgiving, and we are here with most of the town. Let's be thankful for what we have. Not that it isn't great to see you, but what are you doing here? I thought you were celebrating Thanksgiving with your grandmother."

"She wasn't up to cooking a big dinner, so I went over to see her this morning instead." Sipping her beer, she scanned the pub for familiar faces. "Is Faith here? I made her promise she would come, but she still has problems being out in public."

Robbie motioned across the room. "She's over there with Mark."

Nikki smiled at the look on Robbie's face. "You're jealous of Mark. Admit it, you like her."

"I've only been sober for six months. I shouldn't even be thinking about a relationship at this point, but there's just something about her."

Robbie looked into his glass of soda as if he could find life's answers there. "Her eyes remind me of Madison's. I'm afraid I'm just trying to recapture something that's gone forever."

Nikki swallowed the last of the beer in her glass. "Why don't you try just being her friend? She needs someone to help her come out of her shell."

"Sometimes I get the feeling that she wants to be more outgoing, but something holds her back. Do you know what it is?"

"That's her story to tell. Please don't give up on her." Nikki stopped and held up her hand. "Do you hear that? They're playing the song we danced to at prom. Come on, Robbie, dance with me."

Glad for something to take his mind off his memories, he followed Nikki out onto the dance floor and pulled her into his arms, swaying to the beat of the song. The music washed over them, transporting him back to a time before jobs and life and sorrow brought him to his knees.

After dancing to a couple of slow songs, Mark steered Faith back to the table with a hand at her back.

"Thanks, Mark. That was fun. I wasn't sure if I was going to know how to dance."

"You did great. Why would you think you wouldn't know how?"

"I have amnesia. I remember most things but not how or when I learned them. The worst part is not being able to remember who I am."

"How long has it been? What caused it?"

Faith twisted her napkin in her hands. "It's been a little over three years now. I had a traumatic brain injury."

She gulped her wine. "I would appreciate it if you didn't tell anyone. Not many people know."

"Sure, Faith. Why don't you want people to know?"

"When they find out, they treat me differently, like I'm made of glass. They usually stammer that they're sorry and then get away as quickly as they can." She dabbed her eyes. "I've learned to keep it to myself."

Mark moved his chair closer and wrapped his arms around her. "Shhh, don't worry. The people in this town aren't like that. You really don't have to be concerned about it."

"Thanks, Mark. I'm just not ready to start broadcasting my condition yet."

Robbie stared across the room at Faith and Mark, his hand gripping his glass of soda so hard that his knuckles were white. Berating himself for obsessing over someone who obviously had no interest in him, he swung his gaze around the pub, praying something else would grab his attention.

He watched as Adam and Ragan laughed with Fletch Carmichael, noticing the looks Fletch was sending to Nikki. Finally, something to take his mind off of Faith.

Sitting at the bar chatting with Mike, Nikki looked like she belonged, even in her designer clothes and shoes. He could see how someone would be attracted to Nikki.

She was gorgeous and curvy in all the right places, and she had a fantastic sense of humor. Too bad he wasn't attracted to her in that way. They had spent so much time together growing up, it would be like dating his sister. He smiled when she shot Fletch the "quit staring at me you perv" look she'd perfected in high school to rebuff advances made by all the jocks who thought that she would be easy because of her looks.

When Fletch stood and stalked towards her, she pulled Robbie out onto the dance floor and started dancing.

"You afraid of that guy, Nikki?" he asked with a smirk.

"Nope, I can handle him. I just wanted to dance with you again."

"You seriously think I believe that? I saw the looks you two have been trading ever since he laid eyes on you." Robbie turned so he was facing Fletch instead of the wall. At the tap on his shoulder, he set Nikki away from him and whispered, "Behave, Romero."

She laughed and kissed him on the cheek. "Yeah, right. You know that's not going to happen, Newlin." Stepping into Fletch Carmichael's arms as if she belonged there, she danced off.

Whistling, he turned and found Faith watching him, her eyes widening when he returned her stare. He crooked his finger at her, wanting an excuse to hold her in his arms again.

"Who, me?" she asked as she pointed at herself.

"Yeah, you," he replied. *Geez, now I sound like a cheesy eighties movie.* He pulled her into his arms as the song changed to a romantic ballad. His heart sped up when she sighed and laid her head on his shoulder.

"Mark seemed to like you," Robbie remarked, trying to gauge her interest.

"He's nice enough, but he's hung up on your sister. There's no way I can compete with the looks he was giving her tonight."

"He'll get over her once he finds the right woman."

"Obviously, that's not me." She laughed. "Like I'm ready for any kind of commitment, anyway."

He smiled and kept dancing. When the song ended, Adam announced that dinner was ready and for everyone to find their seats.

Ragan whistled to get everyone's attention.

"Thanks, babe," Adam commented with a smile at his wife. "Let's take a moment and remember what we have to be thankful for this year. My family has had an exciting year with much to be thankful for. My life returned to Fairfield Corners when Ragan came home, and I discovered I had a son. I'm now a married man with a beautiful wife and three wonderful kids. My brother-in-law has rediscovered the joy of living and is six-months sober. What else could a man ask for?"

Ragan's voice rang out. "How about your record company signing their first group? Ground Zero is now a part of Sky's The Limit Records."

The room erupted with hoots and whistles, everyone happy that Adam's venture was picking up steam. Robbie watched as Faith slipped out the door, sadness marring her features.

He followed her, the need to kiss her warring with the memory of Madison's face. How can I be attracted to her when my heart died that day? His head warned him to turn around, but his feet kept walking.

Faith stood, leaning against the wall next to the door, her arms hugging herself. She stared off across the parking lot, eyes shining with unshed tears.

"Hey, you okay?" Robbie asked.

Her head snapped around. "What? Are you following me now?"

"You seemed upset. I just wanted to make sure you're okay." He stood in front of her and brushed away a tear from her cheek with his thumb. "What's wrong?"

"Nothing that you can help with. Why don't you just go away?"

His thumb stroked her cheek, and he tried to put how he was feeling into words. "I... Oh, hell." Lips brushing hers, he tilted her head to the side and stepped closer to get a better angle. His lips smashed against hers, his tongue seeking entrance to her mouth, needing more. The feel of her mouth against his awakened his body in a way that he hadn't felt since he lost his wife.

Closing her eyes, she gave in to the kiss, allowing his tongue access as her hands splayed against his chest.

He blinked at her when she pulled away, her breathing erratic. "What the hell was that?"

"Just a kiss. No reason to get all bent out of shape," he replied.

"I'll thank you to keep your tongue to yourself next time. Oh wait, there won't *be* a next time," she emphasized.

"You didn't seem to be protesting too much when your tongue was wrapped around mine."

Exasperated, she stomped back into the pub hoping she could avoid him for the rest of the evening.

Chapter Seven

Robbie rubbed his thigh, the muscles protesting the many trips up and down the steps with armloads of wood. It only took a couple more rounds to finish stacking the cord of firewood Dan had delivered that morning.

According to the news, there was a storm headed for the area with total snow accumulations of ten inches or more and high winds to blow the precipitation all around.

It was hard to believe that the few snowflakes floating through the air now would turn into a blizzard by the end of the day. At least, he had the memory of that kiss on Thanksgiving to keep him warm. Too bad she was an addict. He would have liked to explore their connection in more depth.

After he had placed the last pieces of timber on top of the pile, he turned to take the wheelbarrow back to the shed. His gaze wandered to the house next door, and he wondered if Faith knew what to do to prepare for the storm. Shaking his head to remove the memory of her eyes from his mind, they were so like Madison's that the image made his heart beat harder and increased the craving for a bottle of Jack Daniels to drown it.

He checked his supplies, glad to see plenty of bottled water. If the storm knocked down the power lines, the well pump wouldn't work.

The next morning, Robbie awoke to a chill in the air. He reached out and clicked on the lamp, frowning when it failed to come on. "Damn, I was hoping we wouldn't lose power." Pulling on some sweats and a long-sleeved tee-shirt, he headed for the living room to get a fire started in the fireplace.

The flames crackled as he stared out the window at the house next door, wondering why there was no light visible. He knew the Romero's kept plenty of lanterns in the basement.

Wind caused the flames to leap and dance, throwing shadows throughout the room. The weather radio beeped and began to broadcast the blizzard warning with updated snow accumulations of eighteen inches over the next twelve hours with blowing and drifting likely. *I better go check on her before it gets too bad. She's from California and probably doesn't know what to do during a snowstorm.*

He estimated there was already about ten inches of snow on the ground, almost up to the tops of his boots. He trudged through the snow, exertion making the already strained muscles in his leg burn. Her car was still recognizable, but it would soon be just another lump under the blanket of snow. Pounding on the door, he called out her name and then listened for any response. Two more sets of pounding and yelling brought no indication there was someone in the house. He was prepared for this and pulled the spare keys out of his pocket.

Expecting to see the glow of a lantern and feel the heat from a kerosene heater, he frowned at the darkness and the chill. Playing the flashlight beam around the room, he stomped his way to the bedroom yelling Faith's name.

He found her curled up under the covers, shivering as she slept, passed out from alcohol or hypothermia; he didn't know which. She groaned when he picked her up. Her eyelids fluttered open, and she looked right through him.

"Faith, wake up. Where are your coat and boots?"

Her eyes focused. "What?"

"Where is your coat? I'm taking you next door before you freeze to death. Didn't you hear the blizzard warnings?"

"No." Her hand pushed weakly against his chest. "I can take care of myself. Leave me alone."

Her slurred speech pissed him off. "Did you get any kerosene for the heater?" The chill of her skin convinced him he couldn't leave her to her own devices.

He was surprised at the lack of bottles laying around. From the look of her eyes and her slurred speech, he was convinced she was drunk. He set her on her feet. "Pack a bag, you're coming with me. I have a fire going, and it's much warmer next door."

She stumbled to the dresser and pulled out a drawer. Swaying, she turned and leaned against the piece of furniture with her hand up at her forehead, waiting for the dizziness to pass.

Grumbling about worthless drunks, he grabbed a few sweaters and jeans from the dresser along with socks and underwear and threw them on the bed. He pulled a duffel bag out of the closet and stuffed the clothes from the bed into it. "Can you make it to the living room on your own?" At her nod, he picked up the duffle and strode away.

By the time she stumbled down the hall, he had her coat and boots ready for her. The walk back to his place took twice as long as she stumbled and fell face-first into the snow.

Picking her up out of the snowdrift, he brushed the flakes off of her face, the pallor of her skin making his stomach drop. If she had alcohol poisoning, he had no way to get her to medical help. Tripping over the threshold, he closed the door with his foot and hurried into the living room, wanting to get Faith warm as quickly as possible.

After making up the couch in front of the fireplace, he tucked her in, wondering what her trigger was. He couldn't see himself with her as she was still an active drinker. He had worked so hard to get himself clean and sober and overcome his own addiction.

After stoking the fire, he made up a pallet of blankets on the floor and tried to get a couple hours of sleep.

$\sim$

42

Her scream pulled him from his dreams. Faith thrashed and mumbled, "Please don't hurt me. I'll give you whatever you want."

She jerked awake when Robbie put his hand on her shoulder, a scream tearing from her throat. He winced when her fist connected with his nose. "Shit, that hurt."

Grabbing her shoulder, he shook it, careful to stay out of the way of her flailing arms. "Faith, it's okay. Wake up."

Her eyes opened, and she looked at him. "Robbie? Where am I?" Tears ran down her face, and she sobbed. "Why can't I remember?"

"A lot of people can't remember their dreams." He pulled her into his arms, stroking her back as the sobs tapered off.

"I know," she said as she averted her eyes.

"Hey, look at me, Faith. There's something else, isn't there?" he asked, hoping she would finally acknowledge she had a drinking problem. "A lot of people have a problem with alcohol; you need to admit you have…"

"What? Why do you keep talking about my problem with alcohol? I don't have a drinking problem."

"No need to get defensive. Forget I mentioned it."

"You seriously think I'm an alcoholic?"

"Well, yeah." He leaned back to get a better look at her face. "All the signs are there: the sunglasses, the hangovers, and the time I had to drive you home."

"I wasn't drunk."

"You're lucky you didn't kill yourself driving intoxicated."

Faith stood and glared at him. "I don't have a drinking problem! You might want to ask next time before you assume you know everything." She stomped over to the window and stared out at the snow swirling on the other side of the glass.

Robbie ran his fingers through his hair, knowing she was right. He realized he had convinced himself she was an alcoholic so he could deny how she made him feel. "Shit," he mumbled, "she's right."

A log shifted in the fireplace sending sparks up the chimney, breaking the silence with hisses and pops.

"Faith, I'm sorry." When she didn't move, he stood and walked to stand behind her and look out the window. He frowned when she reached up and wiped away a tear. "If it's not alcohol, what is it?"

She continued to stare out the window as if it was easier to tell her story to the unrelenting snow instead of to him. She closed her eyes and ran her hands up and down her arms. "I have debilitating headaches. The pain makes me nauseous, and the meds make me loopy and knock me out for hours. Bright lights can bring on the headaches, so I usually wear sunglasses all the time."

"That's why you were so out of it earlier. You had taken your pain meds. I'm sorry, Faith." He put his hand on her shoulder. "What's the diagnosis?"

"They're the result of a brain injury, so they don't really know. There's no rhyme or reason to why I get them."

"Come over and sit down. Tell me, what happened."

She sat next to him on the couch. "I only know what I've been told. I don't actually remember what happened. They found me beaten and barely alive under an overpass. I was in a coma for six weeks." She pulled his hand into her lap and interlaced their fingers. "The worst part is, I don't know who I am." Her voice wavered, barely loud enough for him to hear her. "Do you know what it's like to feel that lost?"

His heart twisted at the pain in her voice. Pulling her into his lap, he wrapped his arms around her and held her as she sobbed. "Yeah, I think I do," he muttered. "We've all felt lost at one time or another. I was lost for three years."

"What is your story? I can see the sadness you try to hide."

"We'll talk about that later. We're talking about you right now."

"Fine, if you insist. I'm not letting you off the hook, though. You will tell me your story."

"Scouts honor," he said as he held up his hand with the middle three fingers up. "Now, back to you. So, you have amnesia? Do the doctors think you'll eventually remember?"

"They did at first, but as more time passes, the likelihood of that decreases. It's been over three years, and so chances are that I will never remember more than bits and pieces of my past. The worst part is knowing that no one came forward with any information about me. My story was on all the major network news, but nothing ever came of it. It was as if I didn't exist before they found me."

"That must have been hard, building a new life. How did you end up being an author?"

"I was stuck in the hospital for months with all the surgeries to repair my face. Nikki brought me a Kindle, and I read all day. A story came to me, so Nikki let me borrow her laptop. A couple of months later, I had a rough manuscript. She fronted me the money for editing and I started sending out query letters. It was picked up by an independent publisher and released six months later."

"Wow, that's cool. Anything I might have read?"

She laughed at the thought of Robbie reading a romance. "No, I don't think so. I write historical romance, nothing you would want to read."

"Probably not," he said with a grin. "It must have done well if you can afford to spend the winter in nowhere Indiana writing."

"It was on the New York Times bestseller list for six weeks and makes me enough royalties each month to buy groceries and make a payment to the hospital while I write another book. It helps that Nikki is letting me stay in her family's cottage rent-free. If I had to pay rent, I would need to get a job."

"You're a strong person, Faith. I'm impressed." His stomach growled. "You hungry? I have stuff for sandwiches in the cooler."

"That sounds good."

Twenty minutes later, Faith brushed the crumbs off the table into her hand. "Now that you've heard what little there is about me, I think it's time for you to start talking, Robbie."

"Let me get some wood from the deck, and then we can settle in for a while."

Faith wondered how she was going to survive being cooped up in this house with him—sometimes he was such a self-righteous ass. She couldn't believe he had seriously thought she was an alcoholic, judging her without even asking her about it.

She watched as he moved wood from outside on the deck into the wood box next to the fireplace. After shedding his coat and boots, he knelt in front of the fire and piled a couple of pieces of kindling on the top, using the poker to get them into position. She was mesmerized by the play of his muscles under his t-shirt, her mouth going dry at the thought of what he must look like shirtless. She forced her thoughts back to him being a self-righteous ass. Hopefully, he wouldn't go blabbing her secret to the whole town.

Robbie stood and kneaded the muscles in his thigh, the cold and hours of inactivity making them ache.

"You okay, Robbie? I've noticed you rubbing your leg off and on all morning."

"Yeah, all this sitting around is causing my muscles to cramp. I'll wrap it in a warm towel, and that will help. Make yourself comfortable, I'll be right back." He hung a couple of bath towels over the fireplace screen before limping to the bedroom.

Faith reached up to grab her necklace and remembered that she had put it away the day before. She brought her hand up and ran her fingers through her hair instead, needing something to get rid of her nervous energy. She squinted at the brightness of the lantern on the end table. Grabbing her sunglasses, she put them on and sighed in relief.

Robbie walked out of the bedroom wearing a pair of gym shorts. "Is the lantern too bright? Let me lower that a bit." He fiddled with the flame adjustment, and the light dimmed. "How's that?"

She took off her sunglasses. "Much better, thanks. If you need to turn it back up, just let me know, and I'll put my glasses back on, I'm used to it." She lowered her eyes, still not comfortable being the center of attention.

Robbie turned, and her gaze landed on his muscular thighs, making her aware of him as a man. The sight of the angry red scar on his leg made Faith draw in a breath. "That looks like it was bad. What happened?"

"That's part of my story. I need to start at the beginning, so we'll get to my leg in a bit." He pulled a bottle of water out of the cooler. "Want one?" At her nod, he grabbed another and settled onto the couch.

She traced the scar with her eyes, her hand wanting to sooth away his pain.

Pulling one of the towels off of the fireplace screen, he wrapped it around his thigh and visibly relaxed. "That feels better."

"Tell me what happened." The look of sadness that came over his face made Faith wish she hadn't pressed him about his leg.

"It was just over three years ago that my life fell apart. Before that day, everything was great. I had a wife, a baby on the way, a great job, and a condo two blocks from the ocean. We planned to fly here to have Madison meet the family, but things didn't quite work out that way." He took a long drink from his bottle of water. Clearing his throat, he continued. "I received a call from my boss about a deal I was working on that was supposed to be closed that day. Something went wrong, and I had to take a conference call to sort things out, so I sent my wife to the airport without me. I was going to catch the next flight out and meet her in Indianapolis."

Faith squeezed his hand. "We don't have to do this now."

"I need to do it now. According to my therapist, talking about it will help me move past it." Brushing the hair off of her forehead, he carried on. "I had just hung up from my conference call when the door-bell rang. Two LAPD officers were standing on the stoop, and I knew it wasn't a good thing." Robbie looked into the fire. "They tore my life to shreds with just a few words: 'We regret to inform you that Madison Newlin was killed in a motor vehicle accident.' With that one state-ment, I lost my wife, my child, and my whole life."

"Oh, Robbie. I'm so sorry." She rubbed her hand up and down his back, knowing it was a small gesture, but it was all she had.

As if he couldn't sit still, he jumped up and paced the length of the room, finishing his story as he limped along. "I couldn't face it. Whiskey was the only thing that dulled the pain, so every weekend, I drank until I couldn't feel anything anymore. Eventually, I began drinking after work, which turned into drinking at lunch. After two years had passed, my boss grew tired of trying to get me to help myself, so he did the only thing he could do—fire me. Almost six months later, my savings ran out. I sold what was left and came home. The self-indulgence continued, and I was drunk all the time. No one knew what had happened because I couldn't claw myself out of agony long enough to share. Not wanting to live without her anymore, I even thought about taking all of my sleeping pills at once to put an end to it all."

Faith cried silently, not wanting to interrupt him.

Robbie stopped pacing and moved to sit down, noticing Faith's tears. Pulling her into his lap, he finished his story. "One day, I fell into some glass doors and cut myself up pretty badly. I thought it was fate's way of giving me an out. I was prepared to die—I wanted to—but Logan found me before that could happen. Ragan made me tell her the whole story and she convinced me to get into rehab. That was almost seven months ago."

Knowing the pain of losing a child before they even had a chance to live, Faith hugged him tightly. "I'm sorry you went through that, Robbie." Yawning, she tried to keep her eyes open, but the pain meds were still making her sleepy. She laid her head on his shoulder and closed her eyes for a moment.

Robbie looked down and grinned at her. He ran his thumb lightly along her cheekbone as he whispered, "How could someone walk away from you? Knowing you're not an alcoholic makes it even harder to resist you."

Standing carefully to avoid waking her, Robbie took her over to the couch and laid her down, covering her with the blanket. She looked so beautiful sleeping in the firelight. He sat on the floor in front of her and let his thoughts run free. *What happened before she was found? Why would someone do that to her?* Clearly, it was someone who didn't know her. Even with everything she had been through, she still had such compassion for others.

Staring into the fire, he wondered if she had been put into his life for a reason. Possibly to remind him not to take himself so seriously. His life was getting back on track; maybe he was to help her on her journey. He laughed at the thought. It sounded like the AA stuff was sinking in.

Pulling his phone out of his pocket, he turned it on and took a picture of her angelic face to remind him to keep his ego in check. He quickly made the photo his wallpaper and turned the phone off to conserve the battery.

～

Faith awoke to the smell of beef stew and the swish of sandpaper being rubbed across a piece of wood. She blinked against the brightness of the lantern and fumbled for her sunglasses.

"Here, let me move that over here so it's not quite so bright for you. I had planned on turning that down before you woke up, but I was so intent on the box that I didn't notice you were coming around."

"No problem. I'm used to wearing my sunglasses most of the time." She yawned and looked over toward the windows. "Has the snow let up any?"

"No, not yet. We'll probably be snowed in for a couple of days, if not longer. We're not a high priority for the snowplows since we are the only two out on this road this time of year."

"Really?" She looked around worriedly. "Do we have enough wood to last that long? What about food?"

Robbie sat next to her on the couch. "Don't worry, there's plenty of everything. The pantry is full of canned goods, and there is more firewood under the deck. We'll be fine."

"You're sure?"

"We're used to snow here in the Midwest. There's a snowmobile out in the garage if we have to get out before the snowplows make it through. Be calm, I won't let anything happen to you."

"You must think I'm being silly. Evidently, I have too much time on my hands so I'm starting to look for things to go wrong." She smoothed her hair and wiped the drowsiness out of her eyes. "Too bad I don't have any way to keep my laptop charged. All this free time would be ideal for writing."

Robbie stood and stretched. "You ready for some lunch? Smells like the beef stew is ready. All I have to do is get the biscuits in the oven."

"That sounds wonderful. Is there any way I can help?"

"Everything is done. You can take care of dinner."

"Oh, okay. I hope you like grilled cheese sandwiches. I don't know how to cook anything else." She looked down at her hands, somehow ashamed that she didn't know her way around a kitchen. "I bought a cookbook but haven't gotten up the courage to try any of the recipes."

Pulling her up off the couch, Robbie smiled. "We'll just have to do something about that then." He walked her out to the kitchen. "Lesson number one will be cutting out biscuits."

"Holy cow, you made homemade biscuits? Even with no power?"

"I sure did. Now, you're going to help me finish them. Luckily, we have a gas stove, so cooking is still fairly easy."

"Let's get you started rolling out the biscuit dough." He dumped the sticky mixture out of the bowl onto the counter after spreading around some flour. Placing her in front of him, he picked up the rolling pin and showed her how to roll it out while keeping it a consistent thickness.

Faith struggled to keep her focus on the dough in front of her. Robbie's breath in her ear was stirring up new feelings in her body. She had to concentrate to keep her breathing even. His hands overlaying hers on the rolling pin were sure and steady, guiding her movements.

Handing her a glass, he showed her how to cut out the biscuits and set them on the baking sheet. Before she knew it, the biscuits were in the oven, the smell of them baking filling the air.

Robbie put the dishes in the sink and turned to look at Faith.

"What?"

Reaching over, he brushed at some flour on her cheek with his thumb. "Just wondering how some guy hasn't snapped you up yet."

The touch of his thumb on her skin was like fire across her cheekbone, "You make it sound like I'm a commodity or something." Her cheeks burned as her temper flared. "Maybe I don't want to be snapped up." Sheesh, how could she keep forgetting he could be such an

50

asshat? She turned and stomped across the room to stare out the window. The wind whipped the snow around, and she couldn't tell where the shore ended and the lake began. Her mind whirled like the snowflakes on the wind outside—one moment he was sweet and the next he was insulting her. How was she supposed to survive in such close quarters with him?

Chapter Eight

Robbie looked up and caught Faith watching him use the snow blower to clear the driveway. The last two days had been difficult. Every time he tried to lighten the mood, she buried her nose in a book and ignored him. Maybe it was for the best, having already squandered his one chance at happiness.

He was ecstatic that the day had dawned bright and clear with no wind. The beautiful weather meant he could get out of the house and do some manual activity to take his mind off the blonde currently watching him out the window.

Fighting with the snow blower as he tried to remove a snowdrift, his foot slipped, and he went down hard, banging his head on the frozen ground. He laid there motionless while he tried to determine if he had injured anything other than his pride during the fall.

"Robbie," Faith yelled. "Are you okay?"

He opened his eyes to Faith looking down at him worriedly. "Hey, are you hurt?"

"Nothing but my pride." Noticing her shivering in the cold without her jacket, he stood and brushed the snow off of his pants. "Where is your coat?"

"In the house. I was more worried about you than about being cold," she replied, her teeth chattering.

"Let's get you in where it's warm. Silly girl, running out in the middle of winter without a coat." As soon as they were in the house, he pulled her close. "Thanks for worrying about me." His lips gently pressed to Faith's until she pushed her fingers through his hair and grabbed on.

Moaning, she moved her tongue against Robbie's, slowly, tortuously. Her body pressed up against his, making it hard for him to keep his desire from becoming evident. He watched her pupils expand and her eyelids droop as the kiss continued.

He lost himself in the moment, just like before, forgetting completely about Madison. As the world seeped back into his consciousness, he watched the blush spread across her cheeks, and her eyes opened wider. Those orbs, so full of innocence and need, that looked straight into his soul.

"What was that for?" she asked.

The lights flickered and stayed on. "Looks like we're back on the grid. I better go plug in my phone and call Ragan to let her know we're okay."

Faith stood there and rubbed her lips. They felt like they were swollen and sensitive. That had been one hell of a kiss, not that she had anything to compare it to other than the one he laid on her at Thanksgiving. Grabbing her bag, she carefully folded her clothes and dropped them into it. The last two days had been difficult as she attempted to ignore Robbie's gestures of friendship. Nothing he tried had worked until that kiss. Wow, she still felt off balance.

"What are you doing?" Robbie asked angrily when he spied her bag on the bed.

"Since the power is back on, I can go back to the Romero's. I've imposed on you too long already." She turned and zipped up the sack and slung it over her shoulder. "Besides, I'm on a deadline, and I really need to get back to my book."

"You're not going anywhere. It will take most of the day for the house to warm up after I go relight the pilot light on the furnace. And hopefully, none of the pipes are frozen. Let me check everything out. I'll bring your laptop back with me so you can work on your book."

"No. I should go take care of it myself. I'm sure I can figure it out."

"No. Why are you being so stubborn about this?" he asked. He thought the kiss had fixed everything between them.

She smirked at him, "What? You think just because you lay an awesome kiss on me, I'll blindly listen to you? I don't think so… Shit, I didn't mean to say that."

"You thought it was an awesome kiss?" Robbie grinned as he contemplated kissing her again. "It was pretty phenomenal."

"No need to get a big head. The only kiss I remember was the one from a couple of days ago, so I have nothing to compare it to. It may have been a mediocre kiss for all I know."

His mouth quirked, lifting up on one side, making him look smug. "Believe me, honey, that kiss was definitely not mediocre."

She sneered again, "Maybe for you. I'm going to have to do some research and get back to you."

Laughing, he replied, "You do that. I'm curious to see how I stack up."

Faith grabbed her bag and stomped out of the bedroom. As soon as her boots and coat were on, she was headed for the door.

"I told you I'll go light the pilot light and make sure the pipes aren't frozen. Sit down, and I'll be back in a few minutes," Robbie insisted.

As soon as he walked out the door, she collapsed onto the couch and put her head in her hands. *Holy crap, I've got to get out of here before I fall for him. I'm not in a place to start a relationship. I don't even know who I am.*

Robbie felt like he could melt snow just with his gaze, she had him so riled up. When he stepped outside, he let loose the tight reign he had over his body and the blood rushed south, making him so hard he ached. How could someone as lost and confused about life as he was fall for a someone so fast? He never believed this would happen again, and he wasn't sure of how to respond.

After restarting the furnace, he checked all the piping and was glad to see that nothing had happened. The sooner he got her out of his living space, the better. She deserved someone who was worthy of her. If he had to spend much more time with her, his resolve would be gone, and he'd end up doing something they would both regret.

Grabbing her laptop and power cord, he trudged back to his house where the mood was just as frigid as the temperature outside.

Chapter Nine

Faith hurried into the bookstore. "Am I late? I forgot about having to scrape frost off the windows of my car. How do you deal with it all winter long?"

Cassie took her coat and hung it on the coat rack by the door. "You're not late. We don't start for another ten minutes or so. How about some wine? I mean, it is Words and Wine night." Picking up a glass from the table, she poured the sparkling Chardonnay and handed the glass to Faith, "This is the first time we've had the author of a book here when we discussed it. This should be fun."

"I'm nervous. This is the first book club I've done, so I'm not sure what to expect. You won't be ripping my story apart, will you?" she asked nervously. "I'm not good at taking criticism. My agent says I need to toughen up and get used to it."

"Don't worry. We just talk about the story and how it made us feel." Cassie straightened the glasses and looked over the appetizers, making sure everything was ready.

Ragan breezed into the store. "Hey, Cassie. Hi, Faith. I am so ready for this. AJ was cranky all day; I could use some adult time."

Faith looked at her with concern. "Will Adam be okay with a cranky baby?"

"Oh, yes. AJ is always perfect for Adam. It's irritating how he picks our son up and he immediately stops crying. Don't get me wrong, I think it's great that he's so good with him, but I just wish I knew how he did it."

Faith pushed the heartache down. Talking about babies always made her think of the infant she lost. She crowded around with everyone else when Ragan pulled up some new pictures of AJ on her phone. Fighting back the tears, she turned to the table and reached for the bottle of wine.

Ragan touched her arm. "Hey, you okay, Faith?" She looked into her eyes. "You lost a baby, didn't you? I'm so sorry that I'm going on and on about AJ. When did it happen?"

"A little over three years ago. Usually, I can handle it, but sometimes it just hurts worse than others." She picked up a napkin and dabbed her eyes.

"We need to get together for some girl time sometime soon. Why don't you join us for lunch tomorrow? We can get to know each other a little better."

Faith squared her shoulders, reminding herself that she didn't have any friends here but would like to. "Sure, that sounds nice." The bell above the door rang, letting them know more people had arrived for the book club meeting. "Text me the details."

Cassie clapped her hands to get everyone's attention. "Get some drinks and snacks, and we'll begin."

Two hours later, Faith was all smiles as the last of the book club members walked out the door. "Wow, that was fun, but I'm wiped out. I don't remember the last time I laughed so much." She started picking up plates. "It was nothing like I thought it would be. I can't believe that Mark showed up."

Cassie grinned. "He comes to all the meetings. I love hearing his perspective on the books we read. As a man, he comes at it from an entirely different direction." She gulped the last of the Chardonnay in her glass. "He's cute and single. You two should go out."

"No, I don't think so. I spent some time talking with him at

Thanksgiving dinner. There wasn't any spark there, but I can see how he would be a great friend."

Ragan walked up. "He needs to meet someone. I worry about him rattling around in that big house all by himself. I was really hoping you two would hit it off."

"Sorry. I've got some issues I need to work through before I start looking for a relationship." Faith sighed. "Until then, I'm content with my writing."

"Sounds like we need a full-on girls' day instead of just lunch. Retail therapy and a good restaurant in Fort Wayne. How does that sound?"

"That sounds amazing. I have a phone interview to do at nine, but I'm free after that. Can we go to lunch first and then shopping?"

"Sounds like a plan," Ragan replied. "We can tell you the whole story about Mark. He and I had a thing for a while, but I couldn't deny my love for Adam any longer."

"I sense a great story there," Faith said as she threw the paper plates in the trash. She yawned. "I really need to get going."

"You think that's a great story, just wait until you hear about Cassie and Logan's journey to love. It's a doozy. I hope you believe in the paranormal; otherwise, you'll be a doubter."

"Sounds intriguing."

"How do you feel about pizza?" Cassie asked.

"Sounds good. I should be able to meet you here in the morning."

Chapter Ten

Faith turned and checked out the fit of the jeans from the back in the mirror. The door to the dressing room flew open, and Cassie poked her head in. "Wow, you need to get those. They look fabulous on you, and the teal sweater will look amazing with your eyes."

"I don't know. I wasn't planning on buying anything today."

"If you don't buy them, I'm buying them for you. You not having those jeans would be a crime."

"They really look that good?" Faith pulled on the teal sweater and gasped. "Oh, my. You're right," she exclaimed. The teal color made her eyes sparkle, and the jeans made her look like she had a nice, rounded butt. She looked at the tags. "My credit card is going to scream at me, but you're right, I have to have these. Hopefully, they'll still fit tomorrow after all that pizza I ate for lunch."

Cassie yelled, "Ragan, get over here and check this out. Miss 'I hate shopping for jeans because they never fit' just found the perfect pair."

Ragan pulled the door open wider. "Oh, you're right. Those are fabulous. I'm not finding anything I like today. I'm glad the shopping gods are shining on someone."

Faith changed back into her clothes and headed out of the dressing room area, stopping to put everything on the return rack except for the sweater and jeans. Cassie and Ragan dragged her to the register to pay before she chickened out.

Cassie fanned herself. "It's warm in here. Who else is ready for something to drink?"

Fifteen minutes later, they were sitting around a table in the food court. "So, Faith, tell us about you. You sidestepped our questions about you at lunch. I mean we know about the writing, but what about you? How did you meet Nikki?"

Faith shredded the straw wrapper as she tried to figure out how to start. "I met Nikki in the ICU at the hospital where she works."

"Oh, were you visiting someone?" Ragan asked.

Faith stared down into her soda. "No, I was the patient. I was brought in as a Jane Doe."

Cassie's hand found hers. "What happened, sweetie?"

"I don't know. I was found beneath an underpass, beaten and barely alive. I was in a coma for six weeks."

Ragan scooted her chair closer. "Oh, honey. That's terrible. How did it happen?"

"I don't know. I don't remember anything."

"Were the police able to figure it out?"

"No. I couldn't tell them anything that was helpful, and they didn't even know where I came from." Faith started to stand. "I need to…"

Cassie looked at her. "What do you mean they didn't know where you came from?"

"I don't remember anything. I woke up with no memory."

"Let's go, this party needs to move to my house. We're going to need wine, lots of wine, and chocolate."

Ragan's house was warm and cozy with a lived-in feel that only comes from being a part of a family. After the wine had been poured and they all had large slabs of chocolate cake, Cassie waded right in and asked outright, "So, Faith, you really don't remember anything?"

"Nothing. I woke up with a blank slate for a memory. The police couldn't find any leads, and no one had come looking for me. It's as if I didn't exist before that day."

Ragan set her cake on the table. "So that's why you always seem so hesitant when meeting new people."

"It's like starting over; every situation is new to me. I have no memories to fall back on. Conversations are hard, especially when people start talking about the past and I have nothing to contribute." Faith's eyes filled with tears. "It's scary."

Ragan pulled her into a hug. "We'll be your family. There's always room for one more at our table." Faith couldn't believe her luck, finding two friends so easily.

"I'm shocked I blurted it out like that." Cassie handed her a tissue. "I've only told a few people. I'm actually surprised that Robbie hasn't already talked with you about it, Ragan. I told him while we were snowed in a couple of weeks ago."

"Robbie would never tell anyone unless you said it was okay. He understands about trying to overcome a life-changing event."

"He told me about his wife. Who can blame him for turning to booze."

"What?" Ragan exclaimed. "He told you?"

"Yeah, I saw the scar on his leg and he told me the whole story. The accident, the drinking, and almost giving up. I don't know if I would have been as strong. I probably would have ended it."

"He told you the whole story? Other than family and his therapist, I think you are the only one who he has shared the entire situation with, even how he thought about ending his own life. You must have made quite an impression."

"I don't know about that. One minute Robbie's exceptionally nice and we can talk about anything, and the next, it's like someone else has taken over his body, practically snarling and snapping at me. I just seem to bring it out in him without even trying."

Chapter Eleven

Robbie pulled into the parking lot of the pub, hoping Adam had some ideas about how he could raise money.

Making the memory boxes kept his hands busy, but there was still something missing in his life—a true purpose. The idea he had last night as he sanded wood was tumbling around in his head: A restaurant run by kids to teach them skills they could use to better their lives. Figuring out where to start was his first goal, and he hoped Adam knew someone that could help.

As he walked down the hall, he marveled at what Adam had built —his own record label and recording studio attached to the pub. A picture of Ground Zero hung on the wall. They were the first big name band to sign with Adam's Sky's The Limit records. The office door was open, and he saw Adam showing Skylar the finger placement for a chord. A bassinet was to the side of the chair within easy reach.

Skylar copied his father, trying to hold down the strings on the mini guitar he held. "Like this, Daddy?"

Robbie smiled, imagining Skylar a little older playing the guitar with his dad. He wanted that for himself someday.

"Strum it like I showed you. You'll know if it's right by the sound."

Adam smiled as Skylar played the guitar, pride showing on his face. "Good job, Sky. That's a C chord."

Robbie knocked on the doorframe. "Hey, guys, sounds great."

Adam looked up. "Hey, Robbie."

"Did you see me, Unca Robbie? I played the guitar."

"I sure did, Skylar. Before too long, you'll be playing whole songs.

"You ready for lunch, Sky boy?" Adam asked as he set the guitar in the stand. Let's go out and have Mike get you something to eat while your Uncle Robbie and I talk."

"Okay, Daddy," Skylar chirped. "Can I have grilled cheese and french fries?"

"Sure, buddy," Adam replied.

He walked him out the door, returning a few minutes later. "So, what's up, Robbie?"

"I have an idea for a restaurant but I don't know where to start."

"A restaurant? Don't you know that's the quickest way to go broke?"

"Not a regular restaurant, a restaurant where underprivileged kids can learn real job skills such as cooking, scheduling, and running a business. They can be in charge of the whole thing."

A whimper came from the bassinet. Adam reached in and picked up AJ. "Hey, big boy," he said as he rubbed his hand across his back. "Let's get you changed, and then get you a bottle. How's that?" he crooned as he walked toward the bathroom. "Let me take care of this, and I'll be back."

Watching Adam with AJ, Robbie wondered if he would ever get the chance at a family again. Kids with amber eyes and blonde hair. He shook his head, trying to dispel the thoughts of the family he almost had with Madison. The image stayed, but with a difference. Faith was in his mind instead of Madison. He wondered if he was only attracted to her because of her eyes.

Wandering over to the two-way mirror, Robbie watched as Mike made sure Skylar was eating his lunch. He bowed his head and said a prayer for their souls, both Madison's and the baby's.

Adam put a hand on his shoulder. "You okay, man?"

"Yeah, just thinking what if. What if I hadn't sent Madison on by herself, or what if I had gone with her and left the problem for someone else to solve?"

"Things happen the way they're supposed to. I brought you an iced tea. You ready to get down to business?" Adam asked as he tried to hide his worry for Robbie.

"Sure. I figured you might know someone who would be interested in bankrolling my idea or that is already doing something similar."

Adam leaned against the front of his desk. "Actually, I know someone who might be interested in your idea. Let me talk to him and I'll get back to you."

"That would be great," Robbie replied, wondering who it was.

"You okay, Robbie?"

"Yeah. I've just been feeling alone lately. Maybe I need to get a dog or something."

"That's a good idea. It would give you something to worry about besides yourself. We're going over to the shelter this afternoon if you want to tag along. We picked out a dog a couple of days ago, and he's been checked out by the vet and is ready to come home to us."

"Sure. Won't hurt to take a look." He hoped a dog would help get his mind off the amber-colored eyes that haunted his dreams.

Later that afternoon, Robbie walked along the corridor of the animal shelter, checking out the dogs in each kennel. The Jack Russell was cute, but he wanted something a little bigger. And there she was, a lab mix with huge upright ears. There was just something about that face that called to him. "You're a beautiful girl, aren't you?" He motioned to the volunteer that he would like to meet this dog one-on-one.

"This is Yoyo. She's a Black Lab/German Shepard mix and has a lot of energy but is a really sweet girl."

Robbie knelt down on one knee as she bounced over to him, her excitement bringing a smile to his face as her tongue swiped along his cheek. "Can I take her outside and see how we do on a walk?"

"Sure," the volunteer replied. "We have a large, fenced area so you can even toss a b-a-l-l. I can't say the word. It's her favorite thing and she gets really excited."

After the volunteer had closed the gate, he brought a ball out of his pocket and handed it to Robbie. He grinned at the look in Yoyo's eyes when she spied it. Her butt lifted in the air, and she stared at him with a look that clearly said, "Are you going to throw that or what?"

He tossed the ball across the enclosure and watched as she brought it back every time, dropping it at his feet. "Well, it would be easy to keep you entertained. Just a ball and room to run." He ruffled her fur and laughed when she immediately rolled over and showed her belly. "Look at you, a belly rub slut. We'll get along just fine." He turned to the volunteer. "Can I take her home with me today?"

"Let me check, but I don't think it will be a problem. She has already been to our vet and has had all her shots." He clipped the leash to her collar and handed it to Robbie. "Let's head to the office and get some paperwork done."

After an expensive trip to the pet store, Robbie pulled into the drive. "Well, Yoyo, this is it. Home sweet home."

She barked once as if agreeing with him, her eyes bright as she waited for Robbie to open the door. As soon as he did, she jumped down and sniffed every bush and tree in the front yard before picking a spot to relieve herself.

"Good girl," Robbie exclaimed as he walked her toward the door. "I hope they were right that you are housebroken." He put her in the laundry room where she couldn't cause too much trouble while he unloaded everything from the car. He didn't remember having all this stuff when they had a dog when he was a kid.

After setting up the crate in the spare bedroom, he released Yoyo from the laundry room so she could explore her new home. He showed her the water and food dishes he had filled and set out in the kitchen and then the crate. "This is your bed."

She strolled in and laid down.

"Good girl, Yoyo. Want to go for a walk?" Robbie asked.

The dog bounded out of the crate and ran for the door. She waited patiently for him to follow, looking at him as if to say, "It took you long enough. Let's go."

That was the start of his new routine, walk Yoyo morning and night. She had enough energy that he took her on his run, letting her jog beside him off-leash when he trusted her not to take off. After lunch, it was time to chase the ball for a while. It helped wear her out and kept her from driving him crazy with her boundless energy.

The snow on the ground only seemed to add to the animal's enjoyment of chasing the ball. Bounding through snowdrifts, she always found the thing and brought it back to him.

As the dog chased the ball, Robbie looked over to the cottage next door, waving when he spotted Faith watching them through the window. He wondered how she was doing. She seemed to be avoiding him. After the way he acted the last time they kissed, it didn't surprise him.

As if sensing that Robbie wanted to talk to Faith, Yoyo took off when she heard her door open.

"Yoyo, come back here," Robbie yelled. "Crazy dog, where do you think you're going?" he grumbled as he trudged through the snowy yard towards Faith's door.

"Holy crap!" he heard Faith exclaim. "Where did you come from?"

When he reached the door, he looked into the house and smiled. Faith was sitting on the floor petting and scratching Yoyo, much to the dog's enjoyment.

"Yoyo," he said, trying to keep the smile off his face as he reprimanded her. "What are you doing? You know better than to run off like that."

"She's okay. We were just getting acquainted. Is she yours?"

"Yeah, I adopted her from the animal shelter."

"I'm glad. You needed something to keep your mind occupied. What made you decide to adopt a dog?"

"I went to the shelter with Adam when he picked up their dog. I spotted Yoyo, and it was love at first sight." He rubbed the animal's head as he plowed on. "Hey, I'm sorry for the way I acted that last day.

I shouldn't have forced the kiss on you, and then I acted like a complete asshat about it."

"It's okay. I didn't handle it very well myself."

Robbie grinned. "Let's try being friends. I've actually missed talking to you the last couple of weeks."

"As long as you can keep your lips to yourself," Faith said with a laugh. "I'm glad we had this chance to talk. Ragan invited me to Christmas, so it would have been totally awkward if we still were trying to ignore each other."

"Friends it is," Robbie agreed as he held out his hand to Faith to help her up off the floor. "We're adults. We can do this."

Chapter Twelve

The lights strung on the house and the trees in the yard gave the night a magical quality, the snow muting the colors. Faith stared in wonder; this was her first experience seeing Christmas lights in a snowy climate. "It's so beautiful," she exclaimed.

Robbie smiled at her reaction. "Wait until you see the inside of the house," he said with a chuckle.

The door opened as they meandered up the front walk. "I'm glad you came," Ragan said to Faith, smiling at the picture she made walking up with Robbie.

"Thanks for inviting me," Faith replied as she handed Ragan the gift bag containing the bottle of wine she knew was her favorite. Faith stopped and stared when she walked into the living room. There were so many gifts they took up an entire corner of the living room.

She turned to Robbie and whispered, "Why didn't you tell me? One bottle of wine is not enough. Maybe if I promised a signed book for everyone…"

Robbie grinned. "Do you really think Ragan cares that you brought a bottle of wine or six or ten? My sister loves Christmas and always goes overboard. I've learned to just go with it." He squeezed her hand, "Just so you know, most of the gifts are photographs that Ragan has

68

taken over the last year—nothing that she has spent a lot of money on."

Faith looked up when Ragan grabbed her hand. "Come on, Faith, let's open this wine, and then I want you to meet everyone."

"Give her a chance to catch her breath before you whisk her off," Robbie commented as he helped Faith with her coat. "Wow, you look really nice."

Red crept up her neck at Robbie's words. "Thank you." She wondered how she was going to keep her promise that they could be friends. If he kept complimenting her in that tone of voice, she was going to be in trouble.

"Oh good, you wore the sweater," Ragan said as she grabbed Faith's hand and pulled her toward the kitchen, "and the jeans. No wonder my brother's tongue was practically dragging on the floor."

"We're just friends. Neither one of us wants anything more than that," she protested. Taking the glass of wine she was offered, she gulped at the contents, hoping to cool herself down.

"That isn't what his eyes were saying."

Faith slumped onto one of the barstools. "I don't know how to handle that. I'm not ready."

"I've noticed the way you watch him from across a room. I call bullshit." Ragan topped off Faith's glass. "Just take it slow. You two are good for each other. Now, I've got to play hostess. Go mingle." After a quick hug, she picked up a tray of cookies and disappeared through the door.

Mingle? Faith gulped more of her wine, the thought of interacting with strangers making her feel sick. Taking a deep breath, she stood and swayed, realizing that drinking alcohol that fast on an empty stomach wasn't a good idea.

Picking her way through the buffet, she let her mind whirl with all the names and faces. From the members of Ground Zero to Ragan and Robbie's parents, the wide range of people celebrating with the Bricklins was staggering.

"Hey beautiful, have we met yet?" she heard from behind her. A hand touched her back as a tattooed arm reached around her for a cookie from the plate in front of her on the buffet. She tensed, trying to breathe normally as waves of terror washed through her. She stepped forward, unconsciously trying to get out of his reach as she dropped her plate onto the buffet with a clang.

"Faith? You okay?" Robbie's voice came from her right, her heartbeat thumping in her ears as the panic started taking over. He moved Fletch's hand away from her back. "Sorry, Fletch. She's here with me."

"Sorry, man. Can't fault me for appreciating a beautiful lady."

Turning her so she was facing him, he lifted her chin so she was looking at his face. "It's okay, sweetheart."

She grabbed onto his arm as if to anchor herself to him while she tried to calm her frantic brain. Robbie's stare burned through the waves of panic, bringing her back to the present. She blinked slowly as her breathing returned to normal.

"Oh, I'm sorry, Mr. Carmichael, I didn't realize it was you." Faith placed her hand on his arm. "Nikki mentioned that you were going to be here for Christmas."

He smiled. "Please, call me Fletch. Are you okay?" He held her hand in his before bringing it up to place a kiss on the back of it. "I didn't get a chance to meet you at Thanksgiving, but Nikki had pointed you out to me before you disappeared."

"I'm fine, just a memory sneaking up on me. So, our Nikki seems to be smitten with you Fletch," she said to deflect his attention away from her panic attack. Putting her arm through his, she steered him away from the table. "Nikki is a close friend of mine. I hope you are treating her right."

Robbie stared at Faith's back as she walked with Fletch toward the bar set up in the far corner of the room. The look of panic in her eyes made him want to track down whoever it was that hurt her and cause them some serious pain.

"Hey, you okay, Robbie?" Ragan asked, putting her hand on his arm.

"Yeah, just thinking." He turned and looked at her. "Let me have AJ." He reached over and plucked him from her shoulder. "Hey, little man, what do you think of all this hoopla?"

AJ looked at Robbie sleepily and yawned. "I just finished feeding him, so he's in a milk coma. You okay to hold him for a while?"

"Of course. We can do some manly uncle and nephew things like troll for girls and break some hearts."

Ragan smiled. "Good. Let me know if he gets fussy."

"You think I'm going to let you have him back? Nope, not going to happen. He's coming to live with me." Robbie kissed AJ's head. "Seriously, I'll let you know if I ever get tired of holding him."

"Someday you'll have one of your own. You will be an awesome father."

"Nah. I'll just be the bachelor uncle who spoils your kids rotten."

Ragan shook her head as she walked away.

Grabbing a cookie from the buffet, Robbie walked over to the window and stared out at the starlit sky as he rubbed AJ's back, thinking about the child he would have had with Madison. Would he or she have had her gorgeous eyes? His nose? He would never know.

Chapter Thirteen

The day dawned clear and cold, the wind polishing the ice-covered lake to a high gloss. Just knowing what day it was put him on edge. His hands, at once, sweaty and ice cold as his craving for a bottle of whiskey welled up in waves, each one stronger than the last.

The grief rose up in him as he battled to remain in control. The pictures he had put away in drawers and closets weeks ago called to him. He pulled out each and every one and placed them out where he could see her face from everywhere in the house. Her eyes watched his every move, accusing him of moving on too soon.

Taking a photo down from the mantle, he hugged it as he let the tears flow freely down his face. His heart ached as he stared into the cold fireplace, his eyes seeing her as she looked that last day—so happy and carefree.

"I'm sorry, Maddy," he cried before flinging the photo, frame and all, into the fireplace. Grabbing his coat and keys, he slammed the door on his way out of the house. Grief turned into anger as he drove toward town. Anger that she was dead, anger that he had to live without her. Anger that she was no longer with him but still had such a strong hold on him.

Faith snuggled into the afghan as she sat on the couch sipping a mug of green tea. She had given herself the afternoon off from writing as soon as she finished the chapter she had started that morning. Beaming at the flame crackling merrily in the fireplace, Robbie would be proud of her fire-starting skills today. One match was all it took.

She wondered where he had taken off to this morning. The squeal of his tires on the pavement had attested to his hurry as he drove off. That had been hours ago, so she had gone next door and let Yoyo out and brought her back. The dog had made herself at home and was snoozing in front of the fire as Faith watched an old movie on cable.

The ringing of her phone pulled her from her dream of a family that loved her. The faint glow from the embers of the fire just enough for her to see to grab her phone off the end table. With a yawn, she answered, "Hello?"

When no one answered, she tried again. "Hello?" She heard what sounded like someone stumbling around, tripping over furniture.

"I don't want to live without her..." someone whispered, their voice low and gravelly.

"Robbie? Where are you?" She walked over to the front window and saw his car parked crookedly in his driveway. "Hold on, I'm on my way over." Slipping her phone in her pocket, she pulled on her snow boots and grabbed her coat. With a whistle to call Yoyo, she marched across the yard to Robbie's house.

The worn hinges squealed in protest when the wind blew the door open, slamming it against the wall with a bang. Closing the door behind her, she surveyed the living room, shivering from the cold. "Robbie? Where are you?"

A cold breeze took her attention to the open windows and sliding glass door on the other side of the room. She hurried over and closed everything up, spying Robbie sitting on the floor in front of the sofa drinking directly from a bottle of whiskey. Picking up the newspaper and some kindling, she lit a fire before turning to look at him.

Yanking the blanket off the back of the sofa, she wrapped it around him before kneeling down. "What is it, Robbie? Did something happen to Ragan or the kids?"

Lost in his memories, he stared right through her, the bottle tipping up and pouring more whiskey into his mouth at regular intervals.

"Robbie," she said as she grabbed the bottle out of his hand, "tell me what's wrong. You know this isn't the answer."

He tried to grab the bottle back, but the alcohol had slowed his reflexes enough that she pulled it out of his reach easily. "No. I won't let you do this to yourself."

"She would have been twenty-seven today," he mumbled before dropping his head into his hands.

"I should call Ragan."

"No!" he yelled as he stood up. "Don't call her. I don't want to look at her and remember that she has the perfect family and I'm all alone." Striding past her, Robbie grabbed the bottle and took a long drink. Picking up a picture of Madison, he traced her cheek with the lip of the bottle before he threw it at the wall. The crash of the frame seemed to wake him from his drunken stupor for a moment, his face crumpling as he dropped to his knees and wailed, "She's gone because of me."

"From what you've told me, she loved you very much. She would be heartbroken to see you like this," Faith said as she reached down to comfort him.

He slapped her hand away. "I don't deserve your kindness. I got her killed; it's all my fault." He took another drink from the bottle and then he threw it at the wall where it shattered, whiskey dripping down and pooling along the baseboard.

She dropped to her knees and pulled him into a hug. "It wasn't your fault. It was an accident." Her arms tightened around him when he tried to pull away.

"Why are you doing this? I don't deserve it."

"Yes, you do. Everyone deserves to be happy, even you." Pulling him to his feet, Faith pushed him towards the couch. "Sit down. I'm going to get us a couple of bottles of water, and then you are going to talk to me."

When he made a move to walk away, she pushed him down onto

the couch. "I told you to sit." Reaching into his pocket, she pulled out his keys and tucked them into her own. "I'll just hang on to these until you're sober. The way you parked it looks like you had already been drinking when you drove home. That was terribly stupid, Robbie."

"Is that how I got here? Shit, that was dumb."

"Yeah, it was. Do you realize you could have killed somebody?" She handed him a bottle of water. "Drink that. If you keep hydrated, maybe you won't feel like total shit in the morning."

He grabbed her wrist and pulled her down onto his lap. "Tell me why you're helping me."

"That's an easy one. Because even though you thought I was drunk, you dragged me over here during a snowstorm and made sure I didn't freeze to death." She picked at her fingernail. "Thank you for that." She stood and wiped a stray tear off her cheek. "Do you think you can eat something? Anything to try and soak up some of the alcohol." She made him a sandwich, setting the plate next to him on the floor. "Eat. I've got to run next door and make sure the fire's banked. I'll be back in a few minutes." She brushed the hair out of his eyes and motioned to the plate of food.

"Okay, okay. I'll eat," he replied, his words slurred.

After tending to the fire and closing the doors on the hearth, Faith shrugged on her coat and grabbed her laptop bag so she could work on her book as she kept an eye on him. Closing the door, she made sure she had a good grip on her laptop bag before walking down the steps. The lightly falling snow was making them treacherous, and she didn't want to drop her computer.

She was glad to see Robbie sleeping peacefully on the sofa, the empty plate on the end table. She tried to wake him to get him to the bedroom, but he groaned and rolled over.

Brushing his hair off of his forehead, she wondered what it was like to love someone as deeply as he had loved Madison. She knew she must have loved someone; she had been pregnant when she was attacked. Maybe someday, she would be able to experience that feeling again. Tired of living on the edge of society, she decided that she would start letting more people know about her condition. The few people she'd told here in town had seemed to understand, maybe others would too. Opening her laptop, she settled into the chair and lost herself in the world of highland warriors and damsels in distress.

She looked up when she heard his breathing change, worried that he would choke on his own vomit. Shocked, she realized he was crying in his sleep. "Shhh," she whispered as she leaned over and stroked his face. "It's okay. I'm here. You're not alone." He grabbed her hand and yanked it to his chest, almost pulling her off the chair. She set the laptop down and moved over in front of him, trying to remove her hand from his grasp. Shaking his shoulder to rouse him, she gave up when he smiled in his sleep, the sadness gone from his face. Resigned to spending the night, she lay down next to him and let her mind drift.

The next morning, Faith stretched her arms above her head and yawned. Her heart raced when she realized she was alone on the couch, and Robbie was nowhere in sight. The hiss of the coffee maker helped get her heart rate under control. He was obviously up and coherent enough to make coffee.

Stumbling to the kitchen, she tried to smooth her hair with her hands as she walked. The kitchen was empty. Worried about Robbie, she was relieved to hear the sound of the shower running in the master bath. She fixed her hair with the comb from her purse after washing her face and brushing her teeth with her finger in the guest bath.

The percolating java tickled her nose when she opened the door. Bending over and touching her toes to stretch out her back, she didn't see Robbie walk out of the kitchen.

"Good morning," he said as he held out a cup of coffee.

She straightened, the sight of that man clad in a pair of sweatpants and nothing else making her heart skip a beat or two. "How do you feel this morning?"

He stared at her for a moment before answering. "Not too bad, considering.

"Do you think you could eat some scrambled eggs and toast?" she asked as she pulled a frying pan out of the cupboard.

"You think you can handle cooking eggs? I don't think I can stomach looking at them raw."

"I've got it covered. Scrambled eggs are one of the few things I can cook." She cracked eggs into a bowl, noticing how the sight of raw eggs made Robbie turn a little green. "Go on, go play with the fire or something. I've got this."

He walked out of the kitchen, mumbling something about bossy women.

Poking at the fire, he watched the flames licking at the logs as he frowned at the memory of buying the bottle of whiskey the day before. He needed to get past this need to drown his emotions. He looked up when Faith told him breakfast was ready.

Scooping up the last bite of egg, Robbie noticed Faith watching him. "What? You afraid I'm going to go straight for a bottle?"

"No, but I think you need to talk to someone about what happened yesterday."

"I'll call my sponsor while you take a shower. I'm sure you're stiff from hugging the edge of the couch all night."

"A shower sounds great. I could just head back over to the Romero's, I'm sure you're probably sick of seeing me by now."

"I want you to stay. I'm sure I can find you something to wear." He looked down at his hands. "I really don't want to be alone today."

"Okay, I'll stay."

Robbie watched as Faith bit her lip in concentration while she typed away on her laptop. Yesterday, he had been inconsolable about Madison, but today he couldn't keep his mind off of Faith. Seeing her clothed in his sweats and one of his favorite t-shirts affected him in ways he didn't want to think about. It didn't matter that the too-big clothes hid her curves, just the thought of the material touching her skin made his heart pound.

His sponsor had been disappointed to hear about his slip. He had suggested that Robbie make sure he was around people on his trigger days, such as Madison's birthday or the date she died.

Robbie rubbed the sandpaper across the box, letting the familiar activity take his mind away from his problems. Faith's voice drew his attention back to her. He could hear her talking as if she were having a conversation with someone sitting next to her. Maybe she was trying out some dialogue for her book.

"Sounds like an intense conversation. Is it going in your book?" he asked.

"What? Oh, no. I was just talking to myself...well, to my muse. Sometimes she wants the story to go in a different direction than I do. I'm embarrassed that you saw me; usually, I don't do that in front of people. I've never even slipped in front of Nikki. I guess I feel really comfortable with you.

"I'm honored. Tell me about your muse? Is that your name for your alter ego?"

"No. My muse is an older, grandmotherly-looking woman."

"You actually see her? Aren't you worried about that?"

"No. Something about her makes me feel at home. I guess that's why I can write so well. She brings me a feeling of contentment. I sometimes wonder if she's someone from my past that my mind doesn't want me to forget."

Chapter Fourteen

The day dawned bright with just a hint of chill in the air, unseasonably warm for early spring in northeast Indiana. Robbie knew he needed to explain to Faith why he seemed to run hot and then cold towards her. He was finally ready to admit to her, and to himself, that he was seriously attracted to her. Once you got past her nervousness, she was smart, funny, and her kisses set him on fire so fast he was afraid he would spontaneously combust.

Knocking on her door, he rehearsed what he was going to say in his head. When she answered, all his thoughts disappeared, leaving him standing there stuttering his explanation as to why he was at her door at eight a.m. on a Saturday morning. "Uh, hi, Faith. Can we talk?"

"Okay. So, you're going to be cordial to me today?"

Drawing in a breath, he finally remembered what he wanted to say. "Yes, that's actually what I wanted to talk to you about. How do you feel about fishing?"

"Fishing? Why?"

"It's a great way to spend some time and it will give us a chance to discuss a few things. What do you say?"

She motioned for him to come in. "I'm game. What do I need?"

"Just you. I'll take care of everything else. Meet me out on the dock in twenty minutes. And don't forget to bring a jacket."

Fifteen minutes later, Faith walked onto the dock and stared out across the lake. The sun glinted on the waves, making the water look like it was sparkling.

"Beautiful, isn't it?" Robbie asked, his arms full of fishing gear and a cooler. "That view is the main reason I'm living out here instead of in town. Something about it speaks to my soul."

"It must be wonderful to spend summers here. I can imagine what it looks like with leaves on the trees and boats out on the water. I hope I'll be around when it warms up enough that I can sit out here and write. What a view."

Robbie placed the cooler and the fishing gear in the boat. Turning and looking at Faith, he held out his hand. "You ready?"

Carefully stepping in, she stood still and let her body get used to the feeling of being on the water. "Can we go around the lake before we stop to fish?"

"Sure, we have the whole day and a full gas can, so we could go around the lake twenty times if you want." Untying the ropes mooring the boat to the dock, Robbie pushed off and started the motor. "You ready?" At her nod, he thrust the speed control forward, and they moved away from the shore.

Facing forward, Faith closed her eyes and let her hair blow out behind her in a blonde stream.

Robbie steered the boat with the grace of long practice—his wrist on the wheel, and his legs stretched out before him. Relaxing in the sunshine, he enjoyed being out on the water with no other boats in sight. He slowed down, coming to a stop at his favorite spot to fish. Silence settled over the lake, the soft slapping of waves against the pontoons the only sound. Soaking in the quiet, he closed his eyes and let his mind drift.

"So, are you going to teach me to fish or what?" Faith asked as she poked at the jumble of hooks and lures in the tackle box.

Robbie opened one eye and watched as she examined a brightly colored worm-shaped lure.

"Why would a fish want to eat a bright purple worm?" she mused aloud, her brow wrinkled in confusion.

"I don't know. I just know they do," he replied with a laugh. "Let me show you how to get your rod and lure ready to go." He patiently instructed her on how to tie the jiggly piece of plastic to the fishing line, smiling when she got it tangled in her hair.

"Owww. How in the world did I do that?" she grumbled as she tried to unknot the line.

"Here, let me," Robbie said as he gently extricated it from her hair. "I've got something to fix that," he said as he pulled a ponytail holder out of a bag in the tackle box. "Ragan always forgets to pull her hair back, so I bought a package of these. They've come in handy more than once."

She secured her hair back and smoothed it into a ponytail. "Thanks." She grinned shyly. "Let's get this show on the road. I want to catch some fish."

Teaching her to cast her line out into the water went faster than he thought it would. She seemed to pick it up naturally. They sat side by side. She watched her bobber as he watched her. "You know, I didn't come to catch fish. It was just an excuse to get you out here so we could talk. There's something about being out on the water that is peaceful and relaxing."

"Okay, you talk, I'll fish," Faith said with a smirk."

Casting his line, he settled back into his seat. "I've been at war with myself ever since I met you. From that first day, I've felt this connection to you, and it scares me."

"Why does it scare you?"

"The last time I felt a bond like this, it slipped through my fingers and tore my world apart. I don't know that I could survive that happening a second time, so I push you away." He stared out across the lake. "Your eyes haunt my dreams. They are so like Madison's that I'm afraid I'm just trying to recapture something that's gone forever. I don't know if I'm attracted to you because of that reason or in spite of it."

"Tell me about her," Faith said as she whipped her line back out into the water. "How did the two of you meet?"

"I knocked into her with my surfboard. When she looked up at me, I was a goner." He reeled in his hook and set the fishing rod aside. "She was so beautiful...and those eyes." He sighed and rubbed his hands down his face, trying to keep his emotions in check.

She looked away as if she wanted to give him some space. "I'm sorry that I remind you of her. No wonder you were so grouchy that first day."

"That's no excuse for the way I treated you," he remarked as he pulled the tackle box closer to him and proceeded to dig through the lures. "Anyway, after I picked my tongue up off the pavement, I asked her if she wanted to walk along the boardwalk with me. After dropping my surfboard at my condo, we strolled up and down that span of the beach for hours, talking about anything and everything. Hours went by in what felt like minutes."

"Sounds like a great day."

Robbie stared out over the water, lost in the memory of the first day. "She had a quirky sense of humor, and she always made me laugh, especially when she tried to cook for me. No matter what she did, it was awful. She usually forgot to set the timer and incinerated whatever she made."

"No wonder you're attracted to me, I can't cook either."

"There is that," he said with a laugh. "But seriously, there is something between us, and I am tired of fighting it." Wishing he could see her eyes behind her sunglasses, he went on. "I think we should explore these feelings and see where they take us."

"I don't know if I'm ready for that." Faith quickly reeled in her hook and gently laid the fishing rod on the deck. She carefully walked to the back of the boat and stared out across the lake.

His shoulders slumped. Robbie had sighed before he stowed the fishing gear in preparation for taking Faith back to the cottage. "I'm sorry, I thought you felt the same way. I must have been mistaken."

"I feel it, too," she replied before turning to look at him. "But I'm scared."

"Scared? Of me?"

"Scared of what I'm feeling. What if it's just lust, and I don't understand that? I have nothing to compare these feelings to, so it terrifies me that I'll make a wrong decision." She angrily wiped a tear off her cheek.

"We can take it as slow as you want."

"God, this must be what it feels like to be a sixteen-year-old virgin." She hugged herself and shivered.

"Hey, it's okay. We don't have to do this if you're not ready."

"I need to get past this. You realize you will have to go really slow."

"Yeah," he replied before slamming his lips onto hers. The feel of her mouth against his had his blood rushing downwards as his tongue claimed hers.

When he pulled away, her eyes were glazed and her breathing unsteady. "Not quite what I meant by really slow, Robbie."

"There's just something about you that makes me lose control when I have you in my arms. Can you deal with that as long as I don't take it any farther than some intense kissing?"

"I guess. I just wish I had something to compare these feelings to. No wonder teenagers act the way they do."

He chuckled and gently lifted her chin, so she was looking into his eyes. "Whenever it gets too overwhelming, I want you to tell me. I'll back off and give you as much space as you need."

She wrapped her arms around him and laid her head on his chest. "Maybe I'll be able to explain how all this makes me feel someday. This is much better than not knowing from day to day how you are going to react to me."

He kissed the top of her head, breathing in the scent of her shampoo. "If I start acting like an asshat, you have my permission to set me straight. Never be afraid to call me on it." He drew away from her to look her in the face. "Promise me you'll let me know if I start acting like an ass or if I push you too fast."

"But what if you're going too slow?" she asked with a wicked smirk.

Tugging her back into his arms, he tried to slow the thoughts racing through his brain at her suggestive question. "Please don't tease me like that when we're nowhere near a cold shower."

Chapter Fifteen

Robbie opened the door to the pub and relished the smell of burgers and fries as his stomach rumbled. Adam waved him over to a table at the back away from the crowd.

"Robbie, you remember Brent Halston? I told him about your idea for a restaurant run by at-risk kids and he may be interested in investing." Adam looked down at his buzzing phone. "I've got to take this. There's a snag with Ground Zero's release next week. Mike will get you whatever you need."

"Thanks, Adam," Robbie replied. "We still on for that guitar lesson later?"

"Yeah, I'll see you then. Brent, sorry I have to take off."

"No problem."

Robbie fiddled with the glass of iced tea sitting in front of him. "You were there at Christmas, weren't you? I remember meeting you and then you disappeared."

"To be honest, I don't remember a lot about that night. My fiancée and I had hit a rough patch, and she was there with someone else. It wasn't pretty." Brent drained his glass and motioned to Mike for another soda. "Luckily, we were able to get past our issues, and she's now living in Fairfield Corners full-time."

85

"That's great. I'm happy for you. Adam mentioned you might be interested in investing in an idea I have for a restaurant run by at-risk kids."

Forty minutes later, Robbie whistled as he walked toward the bookstore. He wanted to surprise Faith with the good news. Brent wanted to put up the money to open the restaurant. He felt like he was walking a couple of feet above the sidewalk. Ragan had screamed loud enough that the entire pub heard her through the phone.

He spied Faith sitting on the bench in front of The Book Ends Here, glaring at the phone in her hand. "Hey beautiful, what's wrong?"

She shoved the phone in her pocket and smiled at him. "Nothing. Just a text from my agent. They want my next book four weeks earlier than we previously agreed upon. I'm just trying to decide if that's enough time to get it done."

"Well, how about we take the boat out tonight and have a picnic over on the island? No cell phones, no texts, no work at all." He kissed the frown lines between her eyebrows. "I don't like it when you're upset."

"Why are you in such a good mood?" After a moment, she beamed at him. "You talked to Mr. Halston today. Did he agree to invest?"

"Yes, baby, he did," he exclaimed. "We're scheduled to look at some possible locations next week. Madison's Café will be a reality."

"That's wonderful. A picnic sounds like the perfect way to celebrate. Where is the island? I don't think I've seen one out on the lake."

"It's not really an island, more a peninsula that juts out into the lake. The island has always been the place out there to party or celebrate."

Robbie pulled her into his arms and kissed her, happy when he heard Cassie's voice.

"Geez, Robbie. Get a room already."

Letting go of Faith, he turned and pulled Cassie into a hug. "I'm in such a good mood, I'm not even going to respond to that."

"You got the funding, didn't you? Congrats!"

"Thanks, Cass. Now, I'm stealing my girl, and we're headed for the island for a picnic. I know she agreed to help you out this afternoon, but you'll just have to do without her."

"Go, have fun. I'll manage," she said with a chuckle.

After collecting Faith's purse and laptop, they drove back to the house. Faith skipped up the stairs to change as Robbie pulled fixings for sandwiches out of the fridge. Honey ham sandwiches with swiss cheese and mustard went into the cooler along with mandarin oranges and bottles of water. He found some sparkling grape juice on the back shelf and packed that in the cooler so they could toast his business agreement with Brent. He hoped he wasn't making a huge mistake.

Faith returned wearing jeans and a t-shirt and carrying her jacket. "Do you need any help?"

"Nope, just need your cute behind on the pontoon."

She kissed him and strode out the door, skipping down to the pier. Jumping onto the boat, she untied the bowline after he hopped on and set the cooler down on the deck at the front. He pulled out the key and turned over the motor as she used the scarf from around her neck to tie her hair back. He piloted the boat out to the island. This piece of land was where the older kids and adults celebrated their summer accomplishments, held graduation parties, birthday parties, and even bon voyage parties when the kids grew up and left for college. Now, Robbie continued the tradition by celebrating his good news with Faith there.

With his woman at the wheel, he strode out on the front deck of the pontoon, jumping off to tie up the boat when they maneuvered close to the shore. After shutting off the motor, Faith carried the basket to Robbie, squealing when he picked her up and carried her to dry land.

"Thank you, Sir Galahad," she said with a giggle. "Where do we want to make camp?"

He led her down the beach to a fire ring. "This is the place to celebrate. We partied here for any reason in the past, so I wanted to keep the tradition alive and celebrate Madison's Café becoming a reality."

"I bet you all had some fun times out here. And the view is stupendous."

"It was far enough from our parents that we felt we could let loose

87

but close enough that they could keep us from getting too far out of control." He rooted around in the tree line until he found the tarp-covered pile of firewood. "I'm glad someone replaced the logs. We can cozy up to a nice bonfire. Once the sun goes down, it will cool off quickly."

Faith spread out the blanket and opened the cooler, anxious to see what Robbie packed. "Yum, ham and cheese, and you even brought chocolate." She kissed him on the cheek. "But what are the marshmallows and graham crackers for?"

"You've never had s'mores? Oh, are you in for a treat. There's nothing like them."

"Ooh, can't wait. I've heard of them, but I don't think I've ever had one."

The sun dropped below the horizon as Faith gathered up the garbage from their feast, tucked it into a bag, and stowed it in the cooler. The fire's heat was welcome as the warmth of the sun disappeared. "Is it time for the s'mores yet? I'm dying to try one."

"Hang on, I need to find a couple of suitable branches so we can roast the marshmallows." He trooped through the trees, cutting off a couple of small limbs that would be perfect. "Let me get rid of the bark on the end and then we can begin."

Once he had the sticks ready, he speared the white confections on the ends and handed one to Faith. "Now, no one agrees on the best way to toast your marshmallow. Me, I love them burnt, while Ragan would spend ten minutes getting hers the perfect shade of brown." He stuck his in the fire and waited a moment for it to catch. "When burning your marshmallow, the trick is to pull it out of the fire before it melts and falls off the stick." He pulled his out of the fire and blew on it to put out the flames. "Once it is to your desired doneness, you slap it between two graham crackers with a piece of Hershey's chocolate."

"Sounds easy enough." She took her time and toasted her marshmallow to a golden brown and made her s'more.

He grinned when she took a bite and groaned, "Oh my God, this is so good." Only looking up when Robbie took her hand in his.

"Let me get rid of the chocolate for you." He sucked the sweetness from her fingers, finishing by licking a smear of marshmallow off her cheek.

Their lips met, tongues probing as hands wandered. Thoughts of Madison snuck in as he tried to lose himself in the kiss.

Faith looked at him in surprise. "What's wrong? Usually, I'm the one distracted."

"Just some memories from the past sneaking up on me. It's getting late. We should probably head back."

"Okay. Is there, um, a bathroom out here?" She looked at him, her cheeks red with embarrassment.

"There is an old outhouse over that way, you can just see the roof from here. I'll show you."

"I guess it will be something to mark off my bucket list."

"It's not that terrible. We all take turns making sure it's in good condition each spring. Might as well check if it needs any repairs."

Her hand in his, he led her to the clearing away from the lake where the outhouse stood, the outline of a cabin on the opposite side of the clearing. "Let me check for spiders and other critters."

Faith shuddered. "I'm not too fond of spiders."

"Don't worry, I'll make sure it's safe." He opened the door and used a stick to clear out the accumulation of cobwebs. "I don't see anything crawling around in there, you'll be just fine. Here's the toilet paper."

She took the roll of tissue out of his hand and marched up to the door, peeking around it to check for herself. "Looks okay. Robbie, go back to the boat, I'll be done in a few minutes."

Strolling back to the shore, he stared out across the water. Thoughts of Madison didn't calm his mind as they normally did. Looking down at the wedding ring on his finger, he pulled it off and held it in his hand. The indentation in his skin from the ring made him sad, but he knew it was time to say goodbye. Bringing the round band up to his lips, he kissed it and put it in his pocket. "I'll always love you, Maddy, but it's time for me to move on." He stared out across the lake, feeling lighter than he had for years.

"You okay, Robbie?"

He turned to find Faith staring at him, a worried expression on her face. "Yeah. Just saying goodbye to Madison."

"You took off your ring. Are you sure?"

"It's past time. I'll always lover her, but I'm ready to move forward instead of looking back." He brushed her hair back and kissed her forehead. "You ready to go?"

"Let's head home."

Kicking sand into the fire pit to douse the flames, he smiled. "Yes, let's head home."

Chapter Sixteen

The rain drummed on the roof and dripped from the gutters as Faith shut down her laptop for the day. It had been a couple of weeks since her muse had made an appearance but you wouldn't know it from her word count. She was pleased with her progress. The book would be done by the end of the month if she continued writing as she was. Once she had reached an understanding with Robbie, the words seemed to flow so much easier, as if her mixed up emotions about him had been hindering her progress.

Yoyo's dance at the door and the slam of a car door had her scrambling to put on her boots and raincoat. Robbie was back from town with videos and groceries. She hoped he remembered the popcorn.

Skipping down the stairs, she noticed the way his face brightened when he saw her. Skirting puddles, she hurried to the car and grabbed a couple of bags. "Finally. I thought maybe you got lost on your way back. What did you get for dinner? I'm starving."

Pushing her wet hair off her face, he kissed her forehead and said, "I bought everything we need to make tacos. I know how you like Mexican food."

"What? I told you how I could eat nachos every day, but you didn't believe me."

Their playful banter continued until they loaded the last plate in the dishwasher. Robbie pulled a bag out from the closet where he had hidden it when she went into the pantry to put some items away. He scrolled through the on-demand movies, picking out a couple he thought she would enjoy.

After salting the bowl of popcorn, he carried it out to the living room and set it on the table in front of the couch. Yoyo's head popped up at the smell of the snack, earning her a look from Robbie. "Don't you even think about it, little girl." She put her head back on her paws with a sigh and gave him her pitiful dog face. "Oh, all right," he said as he tossed a piece her way.

When Faith sat next to him on the couch, he cuddled her close and plopped the bowl of popcorn in her lap. "Now, save some for me. Maybe I should have put this in two separate bowls."

"Ha ha, funny guy. Start the show already."

Hugging her, he hit "play" on the remote and kissed her, tasting the salt from the popcorn on her lips. He sat back, and she fed him a piece of popcorn. "So, you're going to share with me?"

"There's no one else who I'd rather share my popcorn with," she replied.

When the music for the cartoon started playing, she screeched in his ear. "Oh my God, I love Looney Tunes. How did you know?"

"I didn't. I hoped you wouldn't mind some Bugs and friends before we watch a movie."

Sitting in the dark watching decades-old cartoons with Robbie felt right. "I bet you and Nikki used to watch these together. She's the only other person I know who is a huge Looney Tunes fan." Faith remarked.

"Of course. Ragan and Cassie and James would be out swimming, but Nikki and I would be in here glued to the television."

They laughed at the antics of the beloved characters, talking about their favorite episodes. Robbie's hands moved down her legs, finding the ticklish spots behind her knees. "Robbie Newlin, what are you doing?" she asked as she tried not to laugh.

"Shhh, I'm hunting wabbits," he said in an Elmer Fudd voice

before he laid her back on the couch and slid on top of her, his weight on his elbows.

"Oooh, my own personal Fudd Muffin," she said before lifting her head to capture his lips in a kiss.

"Fudd Muffin? What?"

"You've heard the term stud muffin, I'm sure. Your Elmer Fudd imitation made me think Fudd muffin."

"Hmmm...Fudd muffin, I like it," he said with a grin before settling his lips over hers for another passionate kiss.

Her mind whirled with all the sensations his kisses stirred up. They had worked their way up to oral sex last week, and she was ready to take it up another level. When he looked at her face to gauge her willingness, she nodded, letting him know she was ready.

"Are you sure?"

"Yes. Can you get on with it please?"

A Cheshire cat-like grin spread across his face as he dealt with a condom. His fingers gauged her readiness as he stared down into her eyes.

She waited expectantly, frowning when he sat up and scrubbed his face.

"What? Why did you stop?"

"You're not ready for this yet."

"What do you mean? I told you I was okay." Her mind whirled with questions. Did he see something he didn't like about her body? Was he rethinking his decision to be with her?"

"You were holding your breath as if you thought it was going to hurt. Until you're one hundred percent sure, I won't take this any farther."

"I'm sorry. I thought I would be okay."

He tugged her onto his lap and kissed her. "I can wait. Yes, I want to make love to you, but you are more to me than just some meaningless sex."

"At least let me take care of your little problem that is poking me." She knelt in front of him on the couch and removed the condom.

"You don't have to do that." His breath hitched when she put her hands on him.

Chapter Seventeen

The weeks flew by as the weather warmed and late spring took a firm hold of the Midwest. Robbie stared out the kitchen window at Faith sitting at the table on the deck, shaded by the umbrella and typing away on her manuscript with Yoyo at her feet. He knew she would work for an hour or two and then take a break for lunch before returning to her book.

He couldn't remember being this happy since Madison's death. As the feelings he had for Faith grew stronger, the ice around his heart melted a bit more each day until he felt whole again. Sitting in the kitchen and contemplating the effect Faith had had on his life, he jumped when his cell phone buzzed and broke the silence.

Reading the text from his real estate agent, his grin morphed into a full-fledged smile as he practically danced around the kitchen. His bid on a storefront in downtown Fort Wayne had been accepted, and closing could happen as soon as the loan paperwork was finalized. His idea for a restaurant concept that taught youth in jeopardy how to run a restaurant was actually coming to life. After sending off a quick text to Brent about the bid acceptance, he pulled the iced tea out of the fridge and poured a couple of glasses. It gave him the perfect excuse to interrupt Faith and tell her the good news.

Yoyo raised her head at his approach, giving a short bark as if to alert Faith to his presence.

Looking up, his girl smiled at the glasses of tea. "How did you know I was about to get up and get a glass for myself?"

After giving her a quick kiss on the cheek, he set the drinks on the table and pulled over a chair. "Guess what?"

"You heard about the bid, didn't you? You look excited, so it must have been good news."

"They accepted the offer, and we could actually close on the storefront next week."

"That's wonderful," she exclaimed as she jumped up and wrapped her arms around him and kissed him. "I have a surprise for you. I've been waiting for the right moment to give it to you, and that moment is now." She opened a file on her laptop and turned it so he could see it. "I had my cover designer do a logo for you. If it's not right, we just need to let her know, and she can come up with something else. You had mentioned that you wanted it to be Madison's Café."

He reached out and touched the screen. "I can't believe you did this. It's perfect. This calls for a celebration. Let's go get a pizza. I'll call and get it ordered, so it'll be ready when we get there."

"That sounds good," she said before kissing him on the cheek. "I just need to grab my shoes."

Watching her walk out of the room, he turned his attention to his phone and dialed the number for the restaurant. When Faith walked back in, he turned off the device and drew her into his arms for a kiss.

"What was that for?" she asked as she dug through her purse trying to find her car keys.

"For being you. Do you realize how much I love you?"

She looked down at her feet as a blush crept up her neck. "I love you more," she said to the floor.

"Say that again. To my face this time."

"Sorry, you know I'm trying. I. Love. You. More," she replied as she looked him in the eye.

"That's better." He bent his head down and captured her lips with his.

After what felt like years, she pulled away, her eyes soft as she ran her hand along his jaw. "We better get going or our pizza will be cold."

"What?"

"Pizza, babe. We have to go."

"Oh, right."

She snickered, glad he was the one feeling just a bit off kilter this time. "Come on, Romeo, let's go."

The parking lot was packed. Everyone must have decided to have Italian that night. His phone buzzed with an incoming call as he put the car in park. "It's Brent. Do you mind if I take this while you get the pizza? He met with the bankers today about the closing date on our loan."

"Sure," she said as she kissed his cheek before climbing out of the car. "Back in a jiffy." Riding the high of Robbie's kisses, Faith entered the restaurant oblivious to everything except the smell of garlic. At the buzz of her cell phone, she answered the call without noticing the identity of the caller.

"Did you think you got rid of me by leaving and changing your number?"

The caller's raspy voice sent a shiver up her spine. She hadn't heard that voice since she requested a new cell phone number right before she left California.

"What do you want with me? I've told you I don't remember. Why can't you just leave me alone?"

"I'm just making sure you haven't forgotten what I told you. If you ever tell anyone what you saw, I will kill them and you."

Her hand shook as she put the gadget in her purse.

Robbie pushed end on his phone, his head whirling with the knowledge that the storefront was theirs and the bank had approved the loan for the needed renovations. He was so anxious to tell Faith about the loan, he was unable to wait for her to return to the car with their meal. Ideas for the renovations shoved all other thoughts out of his mind as he opened the car door.

Faith walked toward him, the pizza box in her hands. He jumped out of the car when he noticed the pallor of her face. "Faith, you okay? Is it one of your headaches?"

"Yeah, I took a pill. I'll be fine in a few minutes."

He drove home one-handed, his other hand holding hers.

Chapter Eighteen

Robbie stopped just outside the open bathroom door and listened to the water fill the tub, his imagination soaking in the details. She would be covered in bubbles with only her head and neck exposed; the old claw-foot tub was deep enough to keep all parts of her covered.

He peeked around the jamb, the open door allowing him to watch her from behind without her knowledge.

Steam rose from the water, her hair curling from the humidity.

The paleness of her skin the day before as they returned from the pizza parlor had worried him, but she looked normal this morning.

The sound of the running faucet almost drowned out the sob that escaped from her throat. "Faith? Baby, what's wrong?" He dropped to his knees next to the tub and reached out to brush a stray curl from her forehead, afraid that she was still experiencing the previous day's headache.

Water sloshed when she sat up abruptly and hugged him to her. "I don't know what's wrong with me."

He wiped at the tears on her cheeks, the fear and worry in her eyes made him want to surround her in bubble wrap and protect her from the world with all its dangers.

Pulling out of her embrace, he stood and dropped his sweatpants to the floor.

"What are you doing?"

"What does it look like? I'm joining you. Scoot up."

He stepped into the tub and lowered himself into the water. "Come here."

She leaned back, settling in between his legs. Her hair brushing against his chest had him hard and aching in seconds. "Sorry, your bare skin against mine... Well, you can feel how that is affecting me."

Shifting so she was leaning on her side, she locked her lips over his and kissed him, running her hand over his wet flesh, dipping lower until she was rubbing along the evidence of his desire.

Groaning, he palmed her breast, licking and sucking the skin of her neck and shoulders as she wrapped her hand around him.

Oblivious to the water sloshing out of the tub, he pulled her on top of him.

Frustrated at the lack of room in the tub, he wrapped her in his arms and stood, bringing them both out of the water before stepping out onto the floor.

She squealed when he picked her up and carried her to the bed, his lips never losing contact with hers.

Looking down at her, the love and desire in her eyes made his breath hitch in his chest. *How did he get lucky a second time?*

"You sure?" he asked as he stared into her eyes.

"Yes," she sighed as she pulled him down on top of her. Her lips found his, and she kissed him, her love for him in every sound she made.

His heartbeat increased as he used his fingertips to explore every inch of her skin while his tongue swirled around one of her breasts, laving the hardened bud before he drew it into his mouth and suckled.

Her hips jerked, and she moaned as she ran her fingers through his hair. "God, how can this feel so right?"

He grinned as he moved to her other breast, giving it the same attention. His hand brushed along her ribcage before he reached between them and found her swollen bundle of nerves.

"Yes," she whimpered. Her hips moved, seeking release from the exquisite pressure. "More, please."

Kissing his way down her stomach, he put her legs over his shoulders and focused on her core, glistening with her arousal.

He brought his mouth to her and sucked, her cries of release spurring him on as he tasted her, his fingers finding her core and slowly moving in and out as she peaked.

He watched as her eyes darkened, the pupils expanding with her desire as her hands grabbed at the blankets. "Oh, God, that feels so much better than when I do it myself."

He laughed and put his head on her leg.

"Oh shit, did I say that out loud?"

He moved up the bed, peppering her body with kisses. "Yeah," he said with a snort. "I love that you finally feel comfortable enough with me to say what you feel, but that was seriously funny."

Grinning like a fool, he captured her mouth with his and finished what he started.

Chapter Nineteen

The soft breeze wafted through the open window, bringing the scent of blooming flowers to Robbie's nose as he diced onion for the potato salad. Thoughts of spending the day with everyone here at the lake on this warm spring day brought a smile to his face. Glancing at the clock, he frowned at the time; Faith should have been back ten minutes ago. She insisted that the signed paperback she had given away through a contest had to be mailed today no matter what he said.

After wiping his hands on the towel next to the sink, he selected her number and set his phone to speaker. When her voice mail engaged, he began to worry, then stared at it as if it could explain why she hadn't answered.

Picking up the knife, he finished dicing the onion and stirred it into the potatoes and mayonnaise already in the bowl. Turning to the refrigerator, he pulled out the container of hard-boiled eggs. Relief flooded through him when his phone rang. Without looking at the screen, he picked up the phone and answered, "Hello? Faith?"

Yoyo looked up from her place on the rug as if sensing Robbie's worry.

"No, it's Logan." After a slight pause he said, "Robbie, there's been an accident."

102

This can't be happening again...

Robbie dropped the bowl of eggs, and it shattered on the floor. He slapped his hand on the counter to keep from falling down. Spots swam before his eyes, and he couldn't catch his breath.

Logan's voice cut through the waves of grief flowing through his body. "Robbie, are you there? Dammit, Robbie, speak to me."

Sliding down onto the floor, he had not noticed that he was sitting on broken glass and cracked eggs. He stared at his phone, willing it to be a dream. Yoyo licked his face and whined.

Robbie wrapped his arm around her neck and hugged her as he struggled to breathe.

"Robbie, Faith's okay. Damn, I should have told you that first. I didn't think. I'm sorry."

"She's okay?" He took a breath, his heart beating hard against his ribs as Logan's words made sense in his scrambled brain.

"Yeah, she is. She has a broken wrist and possibly a concussion. Doc is in with her now."

Brushing the glass and egg off of his pants, he hurried to the door. "I'm on my way."

～

"Faith."

She blinked. Her eyes didn't seem to want to focus. As the hospital room became clearer, she felt someone squeeze her hand.

"Faith, can you hear me, baby?"

"Robbie," she whispered. His red-rimmed eyes locked onto hers, scaring her. "What happened?"

"You were in an accident."

"Is everyone okay? Was it my fault?"

"No, a car ran a red light and hit you while you waited to cross the street. You've got a broken wrist and a concussion."

"Why have you been crying? There's something else wrong with me, isn't there?"

"No, Faith, you're just fine. When Logan called and said there had been an accident, I panicked. I thought I had lost you, too." He sniffed as the terror he had felt in the kitchen threatened to overtake him again. He put his hands on the arms of the chair to push himself up.

Her uninjured hand covered his. "Hey, I'm okay. Come here and lay down next to me."

"What? If the nurse comes in and gives me hell, I'm telling her it was your idea."

Faith smiled and then yawned. "Get over here. I'm tired, and I need to know you're still here. I don't think I could handle it if I woke up alone."

Robbie brushed the hair off of her face as she slept, sending up a silent prayer of thanks that she was all right. After he was sure she was asleep, he brought her hand up and kissed the back of it before carefully slipping off the bed and leaving the room. The soft click of the latch released his pent-up emotions, and he skimmed down the wall and sat on the floor with his head in his hands.

"Robbie, you okay?"

He looked up to find Ragan squatting next to him. "Yeah. I hid my fear from her, and it all came rushing back as soon as I walked out of her room."

"Come on, Robbie, I'm taking you home so you can get some sleep."

"I can't leave her here to wake up alone. She tried to hide it, but I think the idea of that scared her. Who can blame her after what she's been through."

"Are you sure? I can stay so you can get some real sleep."

"No, I'm not leaving her," he said as he patted his pockets looking for his keys. "Damn, I hope my car didn't get towed. I was so frantic when I got here, I think I left it in the fire lane with the engine running, and I need to have someone go out and check on Yoyo."

Ragan dangled his keys from her finger. "Adam moved it for you. I'll head out to the lake and pick up Yoyo, so you don't need to worry about her."

"Thanks, sis." He pulled her into a hug. "I appreciate the offer of a

104

bed for the night, but I'm staying right here until she wakes up. I'll pick up some clothes for her in the morning." Embracing his sister again, Robbie whispered in her ear, "I'm going to ask her to marry me."

Ragan hugged her brother tighter. "I'm so happy for you."

With a bounce in his step, Robbie sauntered down the hall.

～

The alarm on his phone went off, but he was already up and stepping out of the shower. The doctor was releasing Faith later that afternoon. She had finally threatened to get out of the bed and take him home herself if he didn't get a couple hours of sleep.

The ring box in his hand felt heavy as he opened it and pulled out the engagement ring. It was small but perfect for her. Anything bigger, and he knew she would feel self-conscious wearing it. Slipping the ring into his front jeans pocket, he grabbed his keys and headed next door to pack some clothes for her to change into.

Looking around her bedroom, he smiled at the picture of the two of them on the dock that Ragan had snapped a couple of weeks before. Faith was looking out over the lake, but he was watching her, smiling at the happiness in her eyes. Taking jeans and a t-shirt out of the dresser, he laid them out and remembered he hadn't gotten her bag out of the closet.

Unzipping it, he swept the clothes inside, not noticing the small, heart-shaped box dropping into the bag. Packing up the rest of the things she would need, he took one last look around the room, hoping that Faith would agree to move in with him instead of coming back here. He knew how happiness could be fleeting, and he didn't want to waste a second of it.

The drive to the hospital gave him time to plan how he would ask her to marry him. *Should he get down on one knee?* She would love the romantic gesture of a traditional proposal. The sight of the hospital had his palms sweating and his heart thumping. He was sure of his feelings for Faith, and he hoped she wouldn't be overwhelmed with the thought of marriage. Wiping his hands on his jeans, he walked across the parking lot towards his future.

He was oblivious to his shoes squeaking on the freshly waxed floor or the nurses smiling at the look of happiness on his face as he walked down the hall toward Faith's room. The door opened soundlessly and there she was, talking on her cell phone.

"I'm okay, Kendra, really. I should have the rough draft ready for you next week." She looked up at the plop of the bag hitting the chair. "No, you don't need to come to Indiana. I promise I'm in excellent hands."

Robbie bent down near the cell phone and said, "I'll be taking care of her, Kendra. You have nothing to worry about."

Faith giggled at her agent's response. "Here, she wants to talk to you."

He kissed her quickly before putting the phone up to his ear. "Hey, Kendra." He turned and walked over to the window as he listened. "Yes, she's really okay. Just a broken wrist and a slight concussion, nothing to worry about. The doctor is releasing her today."

Faith finished the glass of milk on her tray and then picked up the fork to finish eating the last bite of her lunch. Robbie laid her phone on the table and kissed her, the love shining in his eyes making her blush.

The door opened, and Doc breezed in, clipboard in his hand. "Good afternoon, Faith. How are you feeling?"

"I'm stiff and sore but not too bad. Can I get out of here soon?"

He looked over the papers on the clipboard. "Everything looks good. I'm signing your discharge paperwork, and you'll be good to go home. I'll send the nurse in with home care instructions. You make sure she takes it easy for a few days, Robbie."

"Will do, Doc."

The doctor walked out as the nurse walked in. "I've got your home care instructions. Please read them over and let me know if you have any questions."

Robbie plucked them out of her hand. "I'll take those. She will be following these to the letter."

"Okay then. Do you need any help getting dressed?"

Robbie shooed her out of the room. "I think I can handle it, Marla."

"Pushy, pushy. I should tell your mom, Robbie Newlin," she said with a pointing finger before leaving the room.

"Finally, I've got you alone. I need to talk to you, and I don't want any interruptions." He dug around in his pocket, starting to panic when he didn't feel the ring. "Wrong pocket," he said and laughed nervously. "There you are," he mumbled as his hand closed around the ring.

"What is this about, Robbie?"

He pulled at the collar of his shirt, feeling like it was choking him. Sitting on the edge of the bed, he gripped her right hand and looked into her eyes. "I was just a shell when I opened the door that day to find you standing there. You tried to be nice and introduce yourself, but I was so lost I almost slammed the door in your face."

He wiped his hand on his jeans, nervousness making his hands clammy. "I'm so glad you moved in next door. You brought me back to life." He swallowed, his mouth going dry as he thought about his next words. "Faith, I love you. You helped me believe that I could be happy again."

"Is there a point to this?"

"Yeah, geez, I'm rambling." Moving off the bed, he dropped to one knee and looked up at her. Taking a deep breath, he spoke the words he'd been trying to say. "Will you marry me?" He held out the ring he had been holding in his left hand.

Faith's eyes filled with tears. "I…"

Robbie's heart seemed to stop, waiting for her answer.

"I, um, yes," she said with a smile as tears dripped down her cheeks. "You really love me? Even without knowing who I am?"

"I know who you are. You're Faith McMillan, author and hope-fully fiancée. Your past doesn't matter. I love who you are now." He stared into her eyes as he tried to slip the ring on her finger. The appendages on her left hand were still swollen from her broken wrist, and the ring wouldn't go over her knuckle. "I didn't think this through. I guess I'll have to hold onto this until the swelling goes down."

"Oh no you don't," she exclaimed as she grabbed the ring. "This is mine now, and you can't take it back." Slipping it onto her right hand, she was glowing. "We will put this on my other hand in a few days."

He pulled her into a hug, slowly and carefully, mindful of her injuries. "Yes, we will," he whispered against her lips before pressing in for more contact. He moaned when her mouth opened in invitation, his tongue sweeping in and dueling with hers. His arms tightened around her, only loosening when she gasped in pain.

Pulling back, he looked into her eyes and smiled at the love he saw there. "Let's get you changed so we can get out of here."

They both looked towards the door when they heard a knock. Ragan and Adam walked in with flowers and a "get well" balloon. Ragan looked at Robbie. "You asked her? What did she say?"

Faith grinned. "I said yes!" She lifted her right hand to show off the ring.

Ragan beamed. "You need some help getting changed, Faith?"

"Sure. Honey, can you hand me my clothes, please?"

As Robbie pulled the clothes out of the bag, he felt a chain catch on his finger. The necklace dangled from his hand, the pendant spinning slower and slower. "What's this?" Inspecting it further, he held the charm and turned it over to look at the back. He paled when he saw the numbers engraved in the metal. "Where did you get this? Who put you up to this?"

He backed up, sitting heavily into a chair as he stared at the pendant.

Faith trembled at the look on Robbie's face. "I don't know where I got it."

"What do you mean you don't know?" he demanded.

"They found it in my pocket with a broken chain. I always wondered what the numbers meant."

Robbie stood up, his eyes wild. "I've got to think." He sprinted out the door, not noticing Nikki hurrying down the hall.

"Robbie? What's wrong? Is it Faith?" she asked, worry creasing her brow.

"What is this?" he asked as he held out the necklace. "Is this some-one's idea of a joke? It's not funny."

"What do you mean? That was found in Faith's pocket when they brought her into the hospital."

"This was Madison's," he said as he walked away, his shoulders slumped.

Faith looked up when the door opened, hoping Robbie had come back to explain why he freaked out when he saw her necklace. Seeing it was Nikki, she couldn't hold the tears back any longer.

Adam took Faith's hand. "I'll go talk to him, see if I can't get him to explain what's going on."

"Thanks, Adam."

"You okay, Faith?" Nikki asked, worried about the heartbroken look on her face.

"No. Robbie saw my necklace and freaked out. I don't know why he looked so shattered."

"I saw him in the hall. He said something about it being Madison's necklace, and then he took off."

"Madison's? Why would I have had Madison's necklace in my pocket?"

"I don't know, sweetie."

Chapter Twenty

Faith sat on the porch swing at Cassie's, holding the engagement ring in her hand, wishing that Robbie would come walking up the sidewalk with that grin on his face that she loved. It had been three days since he walked out of her hospital room with her necklace in his hand and a haunted look in his eyes. He seemed to have vanished in a puff of smoke when he drove out of the hospital parking lot. No one had seen him, and her calls went directly to voicemail. *Where are you, Robbie? Why did I have Madison's necklace in my pocket?* The answer was locked in her memory, the memory she would never get back.

Her laptop sat next to her unopened. The book was almost done, but she couldn't concentrate enough to finish it. Every time she opened her computer, she remembered her first encounter with Robbie when she ended up practically plastered to his naked chest.

The swing creaked as Cassie sat down. "I brought you some lunch."

"Thanks, but I'm not hungry."

Cassie's eyes filled with sorrow. "You need to eat."

"I appreciate you letting me stay with you, Cassie. I just couldn't face the house with all the memories." She took a bite of the sandwich and chewed thoughtfully. "I just hope he's okay." She put her hand on her stomach as the nausea hit. "Oh, God." Jumping up, she leaned over the porch railing and threw up what little she had eaten that day.

Cassie rubbed her back and held her hair out of the way as she was wracked with dry heaves. Helping her back to the swing, she felt her forehead. "You don't feel warm. It must be nerves. Let's me call the doctor and see if she can see you today."

Robbie leaned against the railing and watched the clouds roll in from the west. Black and ominous, they promised some nasty weather. Clutching the necklace in his fist, he remembered the day in May that changed his life; the day he met Madison on the boardwalk at Venice Beach.

With his surfboard under his arm, he waited for the parade of Hare Krishnas to go by so he could get back to his condo a couple of blocks away. The rent was ridiculous but being so close to the beach was worth it for a transplanted Midwesterner. He turned to check how much longer he would have to wait, forgetting to watch as he swung his surfboard around.

"Hey, watch what you're doing, big guy."

He turned to face that voice and found a vision sitting on the ground beside him rubbing her left knee. "Oh God, did I hit you with my board? I'm so sorry." He reached down. "Here, let me help you up."

She looked up, and he was mesmerized, her whiskey-colored eyes grabbed his attention like a tractor beam, pulling him down into their swirling depths. Her hand squeezed his, reminding him that he was supposed to be helping her up. They spent the rest of the day wandering up and down the boardwalk hand in hand, talking about anything and everything.

Later that evening, he went back to the shop on the boardwalk and bought the necklace she had admired, having the date engraved on the back. Not that he would ever forget. On their third date, he gave it to her. Once he put it around her neck, she never took it off. He thought it had been lost in the accident.

Two days locked up in this hotel room and Robbie was no closer to figuring out how Madison's necklace ended up in Faith's pocket. He remembered the pendant glinting in the light when he closed the car door after kissing Madison goodbye. *What happened that day?*

After sending off a text to Brent about meeting up, he rubbed his hands over his face, not wanting to stir up all the old feelings but knowing he had to find out the truth. No way could he start a new life with Faith with this hanging over their heads.

The bar was comfortably dim and deserted at such an early hour. Sipping on his iced tea, Robbie glanced at his watch, wondering what was taking Brent so long to get there. He hoped the man had kept his whereabouts a secret. He couldn't face Faith without some answers. Staring into his glass, he wondered what it all meant.

"Robbie? You okay?"

Looking up, he found the man he had been pondering sitting across from him with a drink in his hand. "About as okay as I can be. I need your help."

"Anything you need, I'm here. You know that," Brent said as he motioned to the bartender for another round. "I hope that's tea."

"I wanted to order whiskey but didn't. I have to face this sober." Robbie waited until the waitress left with their empty glasses before he pulled the necklace out of his pocket. "This was Madison's. I gave it to her on our third date, and I don't ever remember her taking it off. I distinctly remember her wearing it when she left for the airport. I know it's hers because of the numbers engraved on the back. They represent the day we met—May 13th. Somehow, it was found in Faith's pocket when she was brought into the emergency room."

"You're sure it's the same necklace?"

"No doubt in my mind." Robbie dangled the chain from his fingers, the pendant swaying and catching the light from the candle on the table. "I remember you said you worked with the LAPD for about six months on a case. I need to get some answers, and you're my best chance. I'm hoping you still have some contacts out there."

"I'll see what I can do. A picture of the necklace would be helpful."

Robbie spread it out on the table, turning it over to show the engraving on the back. "Thanks, Brent."

"You need to call Faith. Jordan told me she's been sick, and Cassie was worried enough to get her an appointment at the clinic."

"Why? What's wrong with her?" Robbie tried to swallow around the baseball that had taken up residence in his throat. His hands shook as he tried to select her number.

"Jordan ran some tests but didn't find anything. Maybe the fact that her fiancé disappeared without a trace a couple of days ago has something to do with it. You need to talk to her."

Robbie took a deep breath and pulled his keys out of his pocket. "Thanks. I owe you big time."

Brent smiled and dialed his phone, hoping that Detective Mickelson would be able to help.

$\sim$

The crack of thunder made her jump, her heart thumping loudly in her ears. The house was quiet. She had finally convinced Cassie that she would be okay by herself, but every little sound was making her mind race. Remembering her hostess's story of the ghost of her gram, she shivered at the creaks and groans of the old house. Turning off her Kindle, she looked up and screamed.

"Robbie?" And there it was, that grin that made her heart thump harder in her chest.

"I'm sorry, Faith. I shouldn't have left like I did but finding her necklace in with your clothes surprised me."

"You believe that I have no idea why it was in my pocket, don't you?" she asked with a tremor in her voice.

Pulling her into his arms, he looked down at the ring on her right hand. "Let's put that on the correct finger." Gently, he switched the ring from her right to her left hand. "That should answer your question. I love you, Faith McMillan."

"I love you, Robert Allen Newlin, more than you know." Running her hand along his jaw, she remarked, "You look like you haven't slept." She tugged him down, and they both relaxed into the couch. "We're together. Nothing else matters."

With his arms around her protectively, he finally let himself relax for the first time since he received the call about her accident.

Cassie found them there, sleeping peacefully. She turned to tiptoe out of the room when she noticed Robbie's eyes were open. "Go back to sleep, everything else can wait."

"Thanks for watching out for Faith while I was gone." He slowly sat up, being careful not to wake his love. "I'm sorry I went off the deep end."

"I hope you told her that."

"Of course, I did. I just can't figure out how the necklace ended up in her pocket. I asked Brent to look into it."

"I'm sure he'll figure it out. Have you talked to Ragan? She's worried about you."

"Yeah, I called her before I got here."

"Good. Now, go to sleep, you look like you need it."

"Cassie, Brent told me Faith hasn't been eating. Has she been back to the doctor? Is something else wrong?"

Cassie sat on the chair. "Jordan stopped by and examined her. There's nothing wrong with her other than worrying about you."

"I didn't mean to make her worry." He pulled Faith a little closer. "She's my life, now. I need to let Madison go, but I can't do that until I know how the necklace ended up in Faith's pocket."

"I'll let you go back to sleep. Dinner will be ready in a couple of hours. I hope you'll stay and eat with us before you head back to the lake."

"Okay. Thanks again for taking care of Faith."

"Anytime, Robbie."

The last rays of the sun disappeared, shrouding them in darkness. Faith was curled up, leaning into Robbie, tucked under his arm where he could keep her warm. "You warm enough, baby?"

"Yeah," she replied as she snuggled closer to him, "this is nice."

"Can I talk to you about the necklace?"

"Sure, honey. I don't know what else I can tell you about it."

"I asked Brent to look into it. I want to be able to put the past behind me once and for all." He kissed the top of her head. "You're my life now, but I need answers."

"So do I. I need to know who I was before the accident. Maybe Brent will be able to figure it out."

Chapter Twenty-One

Brent picked up the CD case and headed out the door, contemplating how Robbie would react to what he'd found.

Robbie stirred the pot of spaghetti sauce before dipping in a tasting spoon. Axe, who was his first recruit, had been resistant to the program at first but discovered a passion for cooking. "Good job," he commented. "That's as good as any I've tasted."

The boy grinned. "Thanks, boss. I'll have Betty put spaghetti up as today's special."

Robbie was proud of what he and Brent had built—a program that kept kids off the streets and gave them the training they could use to get a real job. He glanced at the clock. "Shit, I better get upstairs."

"I heard that, boss," Axe yelled from the front of the restaurant. "That will be a buck for the swear jar."

"You got me." Shoving a dollar in the jar on the shelf, Robbie decided it was time to use the money to get the kids something special. Oh, who was he kidding, he would use his own money. Professional chef's jackets would cost more than the number of dollar bills that could be stuffed in that jar. He took the stairs two at a time, anxious to hear what Brent found out about Madison's necklace.

116

The man of the hour was stirring creamer into a cup of coffee, his face giving nothing away.

"Let's go in my office. Betty knows not to disturb us unless it's an emergency," Robbie commented as he walked across the room.

Once they were both seated, Brent pushed the CD case towards Robbie. "I was surprised at what I found. I'm not sure how you're going to feel about it. Pull up the first file on the CD, there's something on it you need to see."

Robbie loaded the disc into his laptop. "What is this?" he asked when it started playing.

"This was caught by a news helicopter preparing for a broadcast." The helicopter zoomed in on the freeway, swooping low enough that license plates were visible. "See that car heading for the off-ramp?"

"That's my Mustang. You can read the license plate and tell that it's Madison driving." He watched as she struggled to get the car to the off-ramp, a flat tire trying to veer the car back out into traffic. "So, she had a flat tire. What does that have to do with her necklace ending up in Faith's pocket?"

"Now watch the second video file."

"What's this? I don't understand."

Brent cracked his knuckles and started explaining. "This was taken by a police car dash camera about five miles past the off-ramp in the first video. It was recording as the officer made a traffic stop. Watch the cars driving past."

"What am I looking for? Oh wait, there's my Mustang. Madison must have put the top up when she stopped to change the flat tire."

"Take a really good look at the driver of the car. Notice anything strange?"

Robbie watched the video again, this time focusing on the driver. "Why does Madison's hair look so dark? It's almost like she's got black hair."

"There's a good reason for that. I don't think that's Madison."

"What do you mean it's not Madison? That's my car, I recognize the license plate."

"It's possible Madison wasn't the one who died in the accident."

"The coroner identified the remains as Madison. She's dead, isn't she?" Robbie's mind was a whirlwind of thoughts, nothing making sense. "If Madison is still alive, why hasn't she come home to me? No way she left me voluntarily."

"There was no reason to question it was Madison's body."

Brent put his hand on Robbie's shoulder. "Do you have anything of Madison's that might have her DNA? Her toothbrush or her hairbrush? We need to compare it to the DNA from the body found in the car, so I'll need to get an order to exhume the body. I'll get the paperwork to you for your signature."

He continued to stare at the video. "When I packed up my apartment, I threw all of her things in a box and had everything shipped here. The box is in the storage space in the basement at the cottage." He rubbed his hands down his face. "I'll bring it to you when I come into town tomorrow."

Robbie sat motionless on the end of the dock, staring out across the lake. *Madison might be alive? Why wouldn't she have contacted me?* Thoughts swirled around his brain, making him second-guess everything about his relationship with her.

What about the baby? He might have a child somewhere out there.

It had been almost a week since he had provided Madison's toothbrush to Brent for DNA analysis and signed the exhumation order. He felt like he was going to jump out his skin. If Madison were still alive, he just wanted to know why she had let him think she was dead all this time.

The sound of footsteps on the dock behind him brought his focus back to the present. He turned and looked up at Faith.

"Brent's here. He's got the results of the DNA test."

"You okay, Faith? No matter what the test says, we will get through this together." He put her hand in his and brought it up to his mouth for a kiss. They walked up to the cottage hand in hand.

Brent turned when they walked into the room, his face an unreadable mask. "I'm sure Faith told you I have the results."

"Yeah. Let's get this over with."

Brent opened the file in his hand and spread the pages out over the coffee table. He picked up the DNA analysis report and gave it to Robbie. "The DNA extracted from Madison's toothbrush is not a match to the body pulled from your car."

Faith's hand squeezed Robbie's tighter as she searched his face. "You okay, Robbie?"

"After watching that video, I was expecting this, but I don't know how to react. Happy that she didn't die in the wreck? Pissed off that she's been alive all this time and never contacted me?"

"Was she acting strangely before that day? Any unusual behavior?" Brent asked.

"No. We were happy, dammit. At least, I was. Maybe she wasn't, though." Robbie ran his hands through his hair. "I need to know why. I hope you understand, Faith."

"Yeah, I do," she said as she hugged him. "Not knowing will eat at you. I know from experience."

"So, if it wasn't Madison in the car, who was it?"

Brent handed another report to Robbie. "I can't say for sure as we didn't get a DNA match with anything in our databases, but the DNA indicates it was a close relative to Madison, most likely a sibling. Being that her sister disappeared the same day, I'm guessing she's the one who died in the crash."

Robbie gripped Faith's hand tighter. "Is there any way we can find out for sure? I don't have anything of hers that would have her DNA. I don't know what happened to the stuff in her apartment. I vaguely remember one of the officers saying something about taking some of it into evidence."

"I'll check into that. It's probably sitting in an evidence locker somewhere."

"I hate to ask, but can you find Madison? She's not dead, and I have to be able to put this behind me."

"I know a very reputable private investigator. I'll have him try to track her down. If anyone can do it, he can. I'll call him as soon as we're done here." Brent pulled out another paper. "While we were waiting for the results, I started looking at this from the other end. Did you realize Faith was found the same day as the accident?"

"What?" Robbie looked at Faith. "The same day?"

"Wow," Faith exclaimed. "That's some coincidence."

"I've got my contacts pulling the case file. I'll look into it and let you know what I find."

"Thanks, Brent," Robbie said as he shook his hand. "I'll pay whatever it takes."

Two days later, he stared at the folder on his desk. Brent had dropped off the file on Faith that morning. His business partner's warning about the graphic nature of the photos inside running through his mind, he opened the packet and blew out a breath before reading the contents. The images the report planted in his brain were nothing compared to the photos. Her face looked like hamburger—bloody and raw. Hardly recognizable as a human face. He marveled at her strength. To wake up to such physical destruction with no memory of who she was, had to be devastating.

Chapter Twenty-Two

Looking for any lead, Brent had pulled up information on Robbie's Maddy and reached out to some of his old contacts while he waited for the reports on the accident and the autopsy from the LAPD. Madison Renee Miller was the oldest child of deceased parents Thomas and Cecilia Miller. As he probed deeper into her family, he focused on the screen in front of him, not quite believing what he was reading.

Leaning back in his chair, Brent picked up his phone and sent off a text before digging deeper. He printed off the page, perusing the information again just to verify he read it correctly the first time. Engrossed in the paper in his hand, he didn't hear Logan's approach until he knocked on the doorframe.

"Hey, Brent, got your text. What's up?"

"You know Robbie asked me to look into Madison's accident? Well, did he ever mention that Madison's last name was Miller?" He held the paper out to the deputy. "I found something interesting when I started looking into her background."

"Shit, is this for real? Madison was our Sonny? I always wondered what happened to her after her family moved to California." His eyes shimmered. "Damn."

"What are the odds that Robbie would fall in love with your cousin?"

"Somehow, Adam and I were both drawn to Fairfield Corners, so it stands to reason that Sonny would be, too. I want to talk to Adam about this before we tell Robbie." He pulled his phone out of his pocket and tapped on a number.

Ten minutes later in Adam's office at the pub, Adam paced the length of the room and back again. "Robbie's Madison was our Sonny? Are you sure?"

Brent handed him a printout of the database entry showing Madison's connection to him and Logan. "I'd always hoped to find her one day."

Logan clapped him on the shoulder. "You know we have to tell Robbie."

Adam looked closer at the printout. "This says she had a sister. Were you able to find her?"

"No, she disappeared the day of Madison's accident. It's as if she dropped off the face of the earth. Brent and I will do a more in-depth search, so maybe we can find her."

Logan stood in front of the two-way mirror and watched the pub's lunch crowd. "If we're telling Robbie, we might as well do it now. He just walked in."

Brent stood and motioned to the door. "I'll let you two talk to him about this. Just yell if he has any questions. I'll be in the restaurant."

Adam picked up his phone to call Mike, the bartender on duty, and asked him to have Robbie come back to the office.

He opened the office door at Robbie's knock. "Hey, Robbie, thanks for coming back."

"Is Ragan okay? AJ?"

"Everyone is fine. How are things with Faith?"

"Better. We've made progress since I've been back."

"Robbie, Brent discovered something when he was investigating Madison's accident." Adam gently led Robbie over to the couch. "Sit, and we'll tell you what he found."

Looking at him quizzically, Robbie followed his direction and sat on the couch next to Logan. "So, what is so bad that Brent couldn't tell me himself?"

Logan rubbed his hands on his jeans as he thought about how to begin the conversation. "Brent told me you asked him to look into Madison's accident after you found her necklace in Faith's things. While he was waiting on the reports from the LAPD, he started looking into Madison's past." He cleared his throat and continued. "When he pulled up her details, he discovered she had a connection to Adam and me."

"What kind of connection?"

"A family connection. I know you've heard me talk about Miss Hattie and how we spent our summers at her place while our parents toured. Well, our uncle and his wife were part of the group, and their daughter, who we knew as Sonny, would spend the summers with us there at Miss Hattie's. The last time we saw her, she was five years old. After that summer, she moved with her parents out to California. Robbie, your Madison was our cousin Sonny."

Brent shuffled the reports on the table. The private investigator hadn't been able to find Madison. She was just gone. And now, looking at the police report on Faith, he just couldn't wrap his mind around it. She was found about half a mile from the off-ramp where Madison had gotten off the freeway when she had a flat tire. The coincidences were piling up. And the timeframe—she was found about thirty minutes after the accident. Was she there when Madison changed her flat tire? Something just didn't feel right.

"Brent? You about done?" Jordan asked as she stirred something on the stove. "Dinner's almost ready."

He looked up at her. "Yeah. I wish I had something more to tell Robbie and Faith. I'm running into dead-ends on all fronts."

She looked down at the papers spread across the table. "Do you think Madison could have had something to do with Faith being beaten? They have similar coloring. Maybe someone thought she was Madison."

"That's a possibility. I'll have to think about it."

A week later, Brent stared at the report in his hand, not quite believing what he was seeing. He walked across the hall and knocked on the doorframe. "Hey, Robbie, you got a minute?"

"Sure," he answered, looking up from his computer. "What's up?"

"I have some information on Madison."

"Should I call Faith? She's over at the bookstore with Ragan and Cassie getting ready for Words and Wine night."

"No, you should hear this first, and then you can decide how to tell Faith."

"What is it? You found Madison, didn't you?"

Brent didn't say a word and handed the report to Robbie.

Robbie looked up at him in confusion. "This says the DNA sample is a match to Faith. What sample? I don't understand."

"I ran the DNA from Madison's toothbrush against Faith's."

Robbie jumped up and paced the length of the office. "But that means... Holy shit," he whispered. "Faith is Madison." He dropped into his chair as the strength left his legs. "Jesus."

Brent squeezed his shoulder. "You okay?"

"Yeah. I'm just trying to figure out how I'm going to tell her."

"The truth is always the best, believe me."

"How the hell did you figure it out?" Robbie jumped up and hurried toward the door. "Never mind. I've got to tell Faith, I mean Madison."

Thirty seconds later, he ran back into his office and looked around frantically. "What the hell did I do with my keys?"

Brent held out his hand, the keys dangling off his finger. "How about if I drive? I don't want you having an accident."

Robbie's leg bounced up and down during the drive to Fairfield Corners. "What made you decide to run Faith's DNA against the sample from Madison's toothbrush?"

"It was something Jordan said. She made a comment about how Faith could have been mistaken for Madison as their coloring was so similar. I thought maybe they were related, but I was not expecting them to be the same person."

Brent pulled up in front the bookstore, letting Robbie out before driving into a parking space.

Robbie opened the front door and scanned the bookstore, looking for Faith.

"Robbie? You okay?" Ragan asked.

"Yeah," he said with a giant grin. "I'm great. Where's Faith?"

"She's in the office. What's going on?"

He didn't bother answering and took off at a run toward the office.

Faith stood up with a bottle of wine in her hand. "Robbie? What's going on? I thought you were at the restaurant today."

"Brent found something."

"He did? What?" She set the bottle down on the desk with a thunk. "Tell me."

"He found Madison," Robbie stated.

"He did? Where is she? Why did she disappear?" Faith looked at Robbie, not sure why he looked so happy.

"Here, take a look at this," he said as he handed the report to her.

"What does this mean? You just said he found Madison, but this report has my name on it? I'm confused."

"Faith, baby, you *are* Madison."

"What?"

He pulled her into his arms, now knowing why she always felt like she belonged there. "You are Madison," he repeated. He frowned at the tears streaking down her face. "Hey, this is good news."

"I need to think. This is too much…" she mumbled as she raced out the door.

"Faith, wait," he yelled, afraid this news was going to ruin everything if he didn't find out what had her so upset.

The slam of the door was his answer.

⌇

125

Faith sped away, no particular destination in mind. She just needed to get some space and think. The road in front of her disappeared into the distance, through cornfield after cornfield. Her foot pressed harder on the gas pedal as she tried to outrun her thoughts, her mind going back to those first days after she awoke to a world that had no place for her.

The feelings of abandonment welled up, wrenching a sob from her chest. Her mind knew that he would have moved heaven and earth to find her if he had known she was alive, but her heart thumped out a rhythm that seemed to say: *Why, why, why didn't he look for me?*

The end of the road was coming up fast, but Faith didn't notice the signs through her tears. She looked up and saw the guardrail across the end of the road with a big yellow sign that said Dead End. Both feet stomped on the brake pedal as she prayed. She had to stop or run into the ditch on either side of the road. The trough was deep enough that it would probably roll her car, and she had neglected to buckle her seatbelt.

The vehicle came to rest with the bumper just touching the guardrail. As her hands shook, she put it in park and dropped her head against the steering wheel. *How did he not know it wasn't me in that car? How could he give up on me that easily?* She screamed and yelled and cried until she had nothing left.

The purple of dusk had encroached on the car when her attention returned to the present. Her temples throbbed with the beginnings of a headache as she looked around for her purse. Moving slowly and carefully, she checked the backseat and realized it was still at the bookstore. No purse meant no pain meds. There was no way she would be able to make it back to town before the pain became unbearable. Now, what was she going to do?

$\sim$

Night fell as Robbie paced the length of the bookstore. Three hours and nothing from Faith. He was worried. Her purse and cell phone were in the office, and she had no way to call for help if she needed it. Terrified that she had disappeared never to be seen again, his stomach threatened to bring up the sandwich Ragan had made him eat an hour earlier. Cassie's phone rang, and his attention immediately went to her face. His heart hurt when she shook her head no—Logan and James hadn't found her yet.

"I should go to the lake. She'll go there after she's thought things through."

Ragan brushed the hair out of his eyes. "You're in no shape to drive, Robbie Newlin. James and Logan are both out looking for her. They'll find her and bring her back here."

"What if she's gone for good? I can't lose her again."

"Shhh. Everything's going to be okay. You have to believe fate wouldn't put her back in your life for her to leave you here alone."

Faith huddled under the blanket she had found in the back seat, grateful that the sun had finally set. The glinting on the metal guardrail had felt like hot knives searing into her brain. She looked up, testing her equilibrium.

The hard-soled loafers in front of her looked out of place on the gravel road, but she was glad to see them. Maybe whoever was standing there would make a call for her so someone could pick her up out here in the middle of nowhere.

She forced her gaze upward, hoping to see a friendly smile, but she was disappointed to see a scowl on the handsome face looking down at her.

With a click, he turned on the flashlight in his hand, using it to blind her.

"I've been looking for you. How did you end up in the ass-end of nowhere?"

Steeling herself against the pain the bright light was causing as it shined in her eyes, she stood and looked at him square in the face. "Who are you? What do you want?" She knew that voice. "You're the guy who's been calling me."

"Who I am doesn't matter. I want to be sure you will never tell what you saw back in Los Angeles. Being here with *him* may bring your memory back, and I can't have that. I didn't want it to come to this, but you leave me no choice. I'm already damned for killing your sister, what's one more dead body on my conscience?"

He looked back over his shoulder at the sound of a car coming up the road.

The glow of headlights stopped and went out. Faith strained her eyes trying to see who was there without moving. She mentally chanted, "Stay back, stay back," as the stranger returned his attention to her.

She crossed her arms and continued to stare at him, hoping it would spark a memory. Nothing. "What do you mean here with him? I don't understand."

"Here with your husband. Or don't you "remember" that either?" her stalker asked with a sneer. "Don't you think it's time to own up to who you really are?"

The sound of footsteps on gravel took his attention away from her. She stepped back, her head pounding as her vision pulsed in time to her heartbeat. She prayed she wouldn't be sick from the pain.

"Don't move."

The click of the hammer being pulled back brought her attention back up. Her eyes widened in fear at the gun pointing at her head. She couldn't take her attention off the end of the barrel which looked to be the size of a bowling ball from her perspective.

"There's only one way to be sure you never talk."

Faith watched as his finger pulled back on the trigger. The sound of a single gunshot echoed across the empty cornfields.

Deputy Logan Miller turned left onto an unmarked dirt road even though he didn't think Faith would have come this way as it was clearly marked as a dead end. He was not one to do anything half-way, so he continued on. His headlights cut through the darkness, shining off something on the road ahead of him. When he hit the high beams, he could see a car pulled off to the side of the road. He stopped and turned off the headlights, taking out his flashlight to get a closer look. His eyes traveled over the vehicle, looking for the reason it was out here in the middle of nowhere. It didn't seem to have a flat tire, so maybe it had some mechanical issue.

Hearing what sounded like voices coming from ahead of him, he walked slowly toward the sound as he pulled his gun, his flashlight off and in his left hand ready to be turned on and used to temporarily blind a suspect.

The night was dead silent, not even a cricket chirped to break the quiet. His footsteps seemed unnaturally loud as he made his way forward. He could see Faith, her face frozen with fear as the guy in front of him pulled the hammer back on the gun in his hand.

His mind raced, running through every possible outcome in a split second before he brought his gun up and fired, hitting the man in the arm to distract him from Faith.

The gun dropped to the ground, and he clutched his arm, cursing loudly.

Logan cuffed him to the guardrail before bandaging his wound as he called for backup and an ambulance. "You okay, Faith?"

She hadn't moved. Standing there, she trembled as tears ran down her face.

Dropping a blanket around her shoulders, Logan pulled her into a hug. "It's okay, I've got you."

"He was going to kill me over something I can't remember," she whispered between sobs. "Why?"

"I don't know, but we'll find out. Robbie will be here in a few minutes." He led her over to her car and had her sit. Wrapping the blanket around her with one hand, he used the other to dial his cell phone. "Robbie? I've got her. She's okay."

Chuckling at Robbie's response, Logan handed the phone to Faith. "Robbie wants to talk to you. He won't believe me until he hears your voice."

When she ended the call, Logan wrapped another blanket from his trunk around Faith to try and stop her trembling, but she couldn't seem to get her body under control. It was as if being held at gunpoint had broken something inside her. She was glad for the blanket and Logan's arms around her, and she finally stopped shaking as his warmth seeped into her bones. It was as if an older brother were holding her together. When the tears started sliding down her cheeks, Logan pulled out his wallet and removed a picture, smiling as he showed it to her.

"Did I ever tell you about my grandma, Miss Hattie? Adam and I spent every summer at her place while our parents toured." He showed her the picture of his grandmother with eleven-year-old Logan and Adam and a younger girl with pigtails.

She felt like she couldn't breathe. "This is your Miss Hattie?" She gasped for air as the world swam before her eyes.

Tugging her chin up, he looked into her eyes. "Faith? What's wrong?"

"I...see...her..." Sucking in a breath, she continued, "She's... my...muse..."

"Hey, look at me." He put her hand on his chest. "Feel how slow my breathing is, breathe with me. In." He continued five seconds later with, "Out."

She concentrated on the feeling of his breathing beneath her hand, trying to match her breaths with his, her gaze riveted to his bottomless blue eyes that made her feel safe. As her respirations slowed, Logan stared at the photo in his hand.

"You see Miss Hattie?" He stared at her, his frank gaze making her self-conscious. "That makes sense."

"I thought she was just a figment of my imagination, like the characters in my books. Why does my seeing her make sense?"

"The girl with the pigtails is you. Brent found our family connection when he was looking into Madison's past. We lost track of that girl when her parents moved out west." He brushed the hair off her face. "You realize you gained more than just a husband today, don't you? You've also gained a couple of cousins who've been looking for you for years."

She smiled at the mention of cousins. "I have a family." She rubbed her fingers on the picture. "She talks about her boys all the time. She must be talking about you and Adam." Faith smiled at the thought of telling Miss Hattie how Logan still carried around a picture of her.

"It's great that you can talk to her. Most people would think you're crazy, but Adam and I have always lived with things that most people would scoff at. Someday, I'll tell you about them. Even back then, you could talk to ghosts. You spent most of that summer in conversations with Grandpa Jack." He looked up at the distant sound of sirens. "Sounds like the cavalry is almost here."

"Was Robbie mad I took off?" she asked worriedly. "I just needed to get away and think. I didn't realize how much drama it would cause."

"He was mad but only because he was worried. When he found your purse and your meds, he got scared for you."

～

Robbie looked at Brent in disbelief when he grabbed the keys out of his hand. "What?"

"The jingling is driving me nuts. Relax, you talked to her, and she's fine." Brent threw the keys into the center console and shut the lid. "Logan is with her. He won't let her take off again."

"What if this changes everything? What if she thinks I only love her because she's Madison?" Robbie scrubbed his hands up and down his face. "I can't lose her again."

Just before they turned onto the dead-end road, an ambulance roared past them with lights flashing and siren screaming.

"An ambulance? I thought you said she was okay."

"It's not for her. Logan had to shoot someone who was threatening Faith."

"What? Why didn't you tell me?"

"I didn't want you to worry about it. It's over, and she's fine."

Brent pulled up beside the ambulance and put the car in park. "Let's get you to Faith. Logan can explain everything later."

Robbie hurried over to Faith, pulling her into his arms. "You okay, baby?"

131

She nodded, her face buried in his chest.

He smoothed her hair, scanning the controlled chaos around him. His eyes widened in shock when he recognized the guy sitting on a gurney, one arm wrapped in a blood-stained bandage, the other hand-cuffed to the stretcher.

When the paramedic stepped up and asked to examine Faith, Robbie agreed, wanting to have a discussion with Logan about what happened. He found Logan standing off to the side talking on his cell phone. When he ended his call, Robbie stepped closer.

"What's wrong, Robbie?"

"Why was Sam Demond threatening Faith?"

"You know that guy?"

"Yeah, I used to work with him out in Los Angeles."

Logan pulled out his notebook and started writing. "How well do you know him?"

"Just professionally. He was employed by the finance department at Pacific Securities. I usually worked with his boss, but we attended some of the same meetings."

"From what Faith told me, he's been harassing her for months, threatening to hurt her if she told anyone about what she witnessed."

Robbie's heart rate increased as rage filled his mind when he realized what that meant. "What the hell? Threatening her? That bastard knew she was Madison?"

Logan replied, "Calm down, let the police handle it. We'll find out why."

Robbie stomped over to the gurney and grabbed Sam. "What the hell, Sam? You knew she wasn't dead?"

Sam sneered at him. "Stupid bitch saw me talking to Simon Collins. I had to take care of her. If she had blabbed, my career would have been over. The SEC frowns upon insider trading."

"What the hell did you do?" Robbie seized his collar and stepped closer. "Did you try to kill my wife?"

His face emotionless, as if a mask. Sam replied, "I couldn't believe my luck when I saw her pull out of your driveway alone. It was my chance to make sure I didn't go to prison. I was ready to drive her off the road, but she exited the freeway and stopped to pick up another woman. Man, she was a looker. They hugged and laughed after she threw her suitcase in the backseat. I thought I would have to wait for another day, but they pulled off the freeway to change a flat tire. The looker took off in the car as I was taking care of your wife."

Robbie clenched his fist, visibly shaking with the effort to not punch this piece of shit. He needed to hear the whole story first. "You beat her up and left her to die. Did you know she was pregnant? You killed my child." His eyes went flat and looked hard enough to chip ice.

Nonchalantly, as if he was standing in line at a coffee house, Sam finished his story. "Fate was partially on my side that day. I heard about the accident so you can understand my shock when I found out that your wife had died a fiery death, but then there she was on the evening news, unrecognizable but still alive. Damn woman was always with someone, so I had to bide my time until I could get her alone. After weeks of following her, I saw her run out of the store downtown alone. Once I was sure no one else knew where she was, I moved in. I would have been in the clear but for that hick deputy.

"I lost more than three years, Sam. Three years I thought she was dead." He pulled the guy off the gurney, not caring when the handcuffs wrenched his arm back. Robbie's fist plowed into his face, splitting the skin on his cheekbone.

Chapter Twenty-Three

Faith couldn't believe they finally had everything done. The letter in her hand verified that her identity had been restored. She was now Faith Madison Newlin. It had taken six months to get everything sorted out. The life insurance had been repaid, and her new social security card was on its way. She mourned a sister she couldn't remember as she worked to build a life with Robbie.

And now, everything was perfect; the pregnancy test in her hand confirmed it. They were going to be parents. The thought of the child she had lost that fateful day brought a tear to her eye. Wiping it away, she vowed to look to the future instead of the past. Fate had stepped in and intertwined her with Robbie's life a second time.

Her husband was on his way home. The restaurant could run without him for one night. It was certainly good experience for the kids in the program to run things on their own. They knew they could call if they needed to.

It was the anniversary of the day that she returned to Robbie's life. One year ago, she had pounded on the door to her destiny, and Robbie had answered. The sound of keys hitting the dish on the table next to the front door made her smile. She wanted to see his face when he found the test.

His arms snaked around her, pulling her in closer. He nuzzled her ear. "Something smells good." He removed a box from his back pocket. "I have something for you, baby."

Faith's eyes lit up at the name on the box. "Isn't that the jewelry store on the Venice Beach boardwalk? What did you do, Robbie Newlin?"

"Just a little something for my beautiful wife," he replied with a smirk on his face. "Open it already."

Yanking off the box top, she gasped at the necklace nestled in it. "It's beautiful," she said as she removed it from the silky interior.

"You know I wanted to get you a new chain for your pendant, so I had this specially made just for you. See how the links are shaped like the moon?"

"Thank you, sweetheart. It's beautiful. I have something for you, too. Go sit down at the table, and I'll bring it to you."

He took a seat and noticed that the plate wasn't sitting flat on the table. "What the heck?" he said as he lifted it up. When he saw the pregnancy test, he picked it up and looked at it in wonder.

"Say something. Are you happy?"

Robbie pulled her into his arms. "Words can't express how I feel about this."

Faith smiled as she realized this was where she was supposed to be: home in his arms.

About the Author

Romance author, dialysis warrior, furkid mom, and Best Fiends addict. Lover of coffee, 80's music, and all things romance. During the day she carves out writing time in between trips to the back door as doorman to her four-legged furry child. At night after spending quality time with her husband she chips away at her never-ending TBR pile.

Keep up with Hoosiergirl Publishing here:
https://hoosiergirl-publishing.kit.com/df28902ff9

You can find all her links on her website:
https://www.laremenicky.com

Next Up In The Fairfield Corners Series

Last Chance Christmas (A Fairfield Corners Novella) -
From the outside, Brent Halston and Jordan McKenna had the perfect life: the house, the dog, fulfilling careers, and their love. However, Jordan's past refused to leave her alone, threatening to destroy all they had built together. Without explanation, Jordan pushed Brent out of her life, leaving him devastated and confused.

In an attempt to start over, Brent relocated to Fairfield Corners, bought an extravagant house, and mourned the loss of his Jojo. To keep herself from drowning in her own grief, Jordan gave everything she had to her career as a doctor, running the free clinic on the rough side of town. As the holiday season approached, a frantic phone call from Jordan's brother pulled Brent back into Jordan's life, giving them the opportunity to reconnect.

Battling the past and present, their love must survive secrets and betrayal, giving them one last chance to be together.

https://books2read.com/LastChanceXmas

Also from the Lavish Publishing family

SAMANTHA JACOBEY

Rendered (Irrevocable Series Book 1)
Samantha Jacobey
https://books2read.com/Rendered

The end of the world is coming, or so they say, and that puts Bailey Dewitt on a crash course with Armageddon. Orphaned, she and her young brothers find themselves living with their renegade uncle as part of a group of survivalists. She struggles against them, searching for a way to escape, but every discovery only terrifies her more.

For Caleb Cross, the Ranch is a way of life. The members of their group are family, and none should come between them. Smitten from the moment he met Bailey, his choices are no longer easy, his path no longer clear. He wants to welcome her and the twins into their fold and hopes his kin will agree.

But the elders who lead them aren't interested in the troublesome girl. They are plotting for the time they will be rid of her and expect Caleb to go along with their plans - he is after all one of them.

At first, Bailey resists Caleb's charms, but soon must admit that she desperately needs a friend. She has no intention of anything more, but when the elders make their move, she is forced to trust him with her very life.

They both have hard lessons to learn. Relationships built on secrets and lies don't come with guarantees. When the world falls apart around them, some things are Irrevocable.

Realistic sci-fi and romantic suspense will pull you into to the first book of the Irrevocable Trilogy.

Summer's Deceit (The Trilogy Book 1)
Sara J. Bernhardt
https://books2read.com/SummersDeceit

Jane Callahan is a reclusive, seventeen-year-old high school student dealing with the death of her beloved brother. Her home in Southern California with her mother is a constant reminder of her loss and pain. In hopes of escaping her past she moves to North Bend Oregon to live with her father, where she meets a beautiful boy named Aidan Summers.

Jane is intrigued by his looks as well as his unusual ways of attempting to get her attention. After months of uncommon conversation and frustration, an uncertain romance brews between Jane and Aidan, but Aidan has a ghastly secret that could destroy everything.

Get swept away by The Hunter's Trilogy – YA romantic suspense with a paranormal twist.